ESCAPE FROM THE DRAGON CZAR

AN AEGIS OF MERLIN STORY

JAMES E. WISHER

James E. Wisher

SAND HILL PUBLISHING

Edited by: Janie Linn Dullard
Cover art by: Paganus
08051702
ISBN: 978-1-945763-15-1

ON THE RUN

A nya fidgeted and smoothed the front of her best
white dress. She sat in one of the hard-backed chairs
at their little dining room table. A slightly wilted
bunch of daisies resting in a blue vase served as both center-
piece and metaphor. Their whole house sagged like the flow-
ers. The roof needed new shingles, moss covered the cedar
siding, and the shutters hung askew. Since Dad died three
years ago nothing had been fixed. For a man that had so many
friends when alive he certainly had few enough in death.

The delightful scent of baked apple wafted out of the
kitchen, making her mouth water. Her mother puttered about
at the oven, getting everything ready. Anya loved baked apples
and every year on her birthday Mom broke into their savings
to buy the costly spices to fix one for her.

Hard slats dug into her back, forcing her to shift again.
From the kitchen came a curse followed by the oven door
slamming.

"Are you okay, Mom?" Anya got up and took a step toward

the kitchen.

Her mother appeared in the open door. She smiled and the fine lines around her eyes crinkled and gray-blond hair spilled down over her blue eyes. "I'm fine, *kiska*. Sit down, this is your special day."

Anya sighed and returned to her uncomfortable chair. "Mom, I'm too old for you to call me kitten."

Her mother brushed a strand of hair out of her eyes. "You'll always be my little kiska, even when you're as old and gray as me."

She smiled as her mother disappeared into the kitchen to finish the baked apple. Listening to her talk you'd think Mom was ancient rather than just forty. Anya licked her lips and pictured the apple coming out of the oven. She ran a finger over the battered fork in front of her. Not much longer now. Maybe they could finish before anyone showed up.

Normally this was her favorite day of the year, but this year they expected a special, if unwelcome, guest. One of the czar's White Witches would arrive soon to test Anya. If the test revealed wizard potential, she'd be taken to New St. Petersburg to meet the czar. She shuddered at the thought of having to leave their little village and never seeing her mother again.

All the girls in the Empire of the Dragon Czar got this visit on their eighteenth birthdays. And they'd all heard the stories as well. Stories of girls taken away and never being heard from again. Anya didn't know how much credit to give the stories. Most of them sounded like nonsense, but people did vanish and they did it often enough that it had become an almost normal part of life in the Empire.

Mom emerged from the kitchen in a swirl of green skirt. She held a steaming red apple dripping with honey. Anya grinned.

"Ta-da." She set the plate in front of Anya and kissed her forehead. "Happy birthday, kiska."

"Thanks, Mom." Anya picked up her fork and knife as her mother rounded the table.

She breathed in the scent of cinnamon and nutmeg. Both spices cost more than they spent on food in a week, but today only they splurged. She almost felt guilty. Almost.

Anya cut a chunk out of the warm, soft apple, taking her time and savoring the moment. The first bite was halfway to her mouth when someone knocked on the door. Before either of them could get up to answer it, the door opened and a woman in white robes with hair as pale as fresh snow stepped inside like she owned the place.

Mom scrambled to her feet and Anya quickly joined her, her special treat forgotten.

"Welcome, Mistress," Mom said. "May I offer you—"

The White Witch held up a hand and Mom fell silent. "This will not take long." Her voice was as cold as a midwinter night.

From the folds of her robe the witch withdrew a length of smooth wood inset with six clear gems. She strode from the door to their table and held the rod out to Anya, who stared at the smooth, dark length of wood.

"Don't look at it, fool, take it," the witch said.

Anya grasped the device with a trembling hand and held her breath. She said a silent prayer to any god that might be listening. Please, oh please, let nothing happen. Let me fail this test and get on with the rest of my boring life.

As if to mock her, the first gem burst into light. Anya's heart sank. She had magic in her blood. Now her life was over.

A second gem lit up, then a third and fourth. When another half a minute passed and nothing happened, the witch snatched the rod out of her hand.

"Congratulations, sister. You will have the honor of joining our ranks in glorious service to the czar. I trust your bag is prepared in accordance with the law?"

"Yes, Mistress." Somehow Anya forced the words past her numb lips.

"Well don't just stand there, girl. Go get it. I have twenty more stops to make today."

Mind racing and rigid with fear, Anya walked up the stairs to her room on the second floor. She pushed the door open and looked for the last time at the soft gray blanket that covered her narrow bed, the handful of stuffed animals her father had bought her before he died, and last, the ancient carved wardrobe, originally owned by her great-grandmother who had left it to Anya when she died. All Anya's meager possessions fit in it with room to spare. She'd never see any of them again.

Her battered leather valise sat on the floor in front of the bed. She staggered over to it like a clockwork figure from a story and picked it up. Silent tears ran down her face.

Anya looked out the single narrow window. She could jump out, but the fall wouldn't kill her. Maybe she'd break a leg, but that wouldn't spare her. If anything it would simply annoy the witch and maybe bring down some sort of punishment on her mother.

"Hurry up, girl!"

How Anya would have liked to strangle the witch. Who did she think she was, turning Anya's life upside down like this? She wiped her eyes and turned her back on everything she'd ever known.

At the bottom of the steps the witch stood, toe tapping and hard, pale eyes glaring up at Anya. Beyond her on the opposite side of the table her mother wrung her hands and watched as Anya went down the steps.

"Finally. Come along." The witch marched toward the door.

Anya fell in behind her. Her gaze darted to her mother. She wanted to ask for advice, reassurance, anything to delay the inevitable.

"Be brave, kiska. Everything will work out."

How could everything work out? She was being dragged away from her home, practically kidnapped by this woman in white.

The witch stopped in the doorway and turned back. "Hurry up, girl. We haven't go—"

A straight, double-edged dagger drove into the witch's throat. Blood shot out, glittering in the air like floating rubies.

Anya dropped her bag and brought her hands to her mouth. The witch stared in total disbelief, a hand clamped to her neck in a vain attempt to stop her life from gushing out.

At last she collapsed, revealing a broad, paunchy man with a heavy gray beard behind her holding a dripping knife. Anya stared first at the dead witch then at her murderer. She felt like she should say something, but her mouth refused to work.

The stranger stepped over the dead witch and into their house, the bloody knife still clutched in his hand. Anya scrambled away from him.

Were they next?

Suddenly a trip to see the czar didn't seem so terrible.

* * *

Her mother's arms around her shook Anya out of her stupor. How long had she just stared like a frightened rabbit?

5

"It's okay, kiska. This is an old friend of your father's. Fedor is a member of the resistance. He's going to help us escape."

"And we'd best be about it," Fedor said. He'd sheathed his knife and grabbed the dead witch by the ankle. "Is everything prepared as we discussed, Sasha?"

"Yes, we're ready," her mother said.

Fedor dragged the witch into the dining room and dropped her leg. Next he flipped the table over and smashed it to pieces. Anya's baked apple splattered on the floor.

"What's he doing?" Anya watched, horrified, as the strange man set about destroying their meager furniture. Maybe this was all a nightmare and she'd wake up in her warm bed and get to start the day over.

Mom let her go and came around to look her in the eye. "I'm sorry it had to be this way, Anya, but if we're to have any hope of getting away we must do this."

"Take her outside, Sasha," Fedor said. "I won't be much longer."

Mom reached into the hall closet and came out with a bag of her own. Anya stared at it. Had her mother planned all this? When? How? How did her mother know members of the resistance? She worked in the pillow factory for heaven's sake.

Her mother thrust her bag into her arms, grabbed her hand, and half guided, half dragged her out into the yard.

A gleaming white van long enough to carry fifteen people sat in the center of the driveway. A scale-covered fist decorated the door. It had to be the witch's transport. That van would have carried her away from everything she knew.

Anya looked back at their little house. In the kitchen window a flash of orange appeared. Fedor hustled out the front door. For a big man he moved right along.

6

"Hurry," he said. "The fire will bring the authorities soon enough."

"Fire?" Anya noticed the smoke an instant after she spoke. "Why?"

Mother tugged on her hand and they followed Fedor up the driveway and out to the rough dirt road. No one said anything as they quick marched through the gravel.

Anya glanced over her shoulder. They'd covered a quarter mile, but she could see the smoke billowing up as their house burned.

She dug in her heels. "Someone tell me what's going on."

Her mother stopped and faced her, her eyes beyond sad. "I wouldn't let them have you too, Anya. Servants of the czar took your father from us. I refused to give up any more to them."

"The clock is ticking, Sasha." Fedor had stopped a little ways up the road. "We need to reach the truck. You can tell her everything then."

"Of course." Mom looked deep into Anya's eyes. "Will you trust me a little longer, kiska?"

Anya trusted her mother to the end of the world. She nodded and they hurried on their way. A mile from home they turned down a rutted side path—calling it a road seemed far too generous. They'd barely gone a hundred yards when they reached a flatbed dual-wheel truck that used to be red, but now had more rust than anything. The bed of the truck held a load of summer vegetables piled into tan baskets.

Fedor yanked twice on the tailgate before it came free. He held out his hand and helped Mom up into the back. Once she was up he looked at Anya and held his hand out to her.

Should she trust this man? All she knew was that he wasn't

afraid to kill. The image of blood gushing out of the witch's neck still burned in her memory.

She steeled herself. Mom trusted him and she trusted her mother. Anya put her hand in his calloused palm. With Fedor's help she clambered up into the back of the truck.

"Help me, Anya." Her mother had bent over and grabbed the handle of a basket filled with zucchini.

Together they shifted the container to reveal a small hiding space in the middle of the vegetables. She followed her mother inside and Fedor shoved the basket into place leaving them in the shadowy interior. The grassy scent of fresh-picked vegetables surrounded them. The only light came from a few gaps in the basket stack. If anyone looked close they'd see Anya and her mother hiding, but that seemed unlikely.

As unlikely as a White Witch being murdered on their front porch and the two of them ending up on the run with a man she'd never seen before. Anya needed answers before her head exploded.

Outside, the truck rumbled to life, jerked, and they started moving.

"You said you'd tell me everything," Anya said. She couldn't see her mother's face in the dark, but she looked in that direction. "I'm listening."

* * *

Anya used her hands and feet to try and brace herself as the truck rattled through ruts and potholes. The engine went from roar to rattle to screech and she feared they might end up stranded god knew where. An especially hard lurch sent her sliding into her mother; only the cloth of her dress prevented her from getting splinters in her butt. There had to be worse ways to travel, but in that moment she couldn't think of one.

In the dark beside her, Mom blew out a sigh. "Where should I begin?"

"At the beginning," Anya said. "How did you ever get mixed up with the resistance?"

"It wasn't that we wanted to, you know. Life in the Empire is hard, but your father and I managed and were happy. Then I got pregnant."

"With me?"

"That's right. It came as a shock since the doctor told me I'd never be able to have children. We thought of you as our little miracle. Five months into the pregnancy the doctor announced I was going to have a girl. I was so excited, then I remembered my grandmother."

"Great-Grandma Catherine? What made you think of her?" Anya hadn't known her maternal great-grandmother beyond the fact that she left her a wardrobe that was now so much firewood.

"My grandmother had wizard potential, like you. The White Witches came for her when she turned eighteen. She'd already had my mother, but that bought no consideration from the witches."

"I still don't understand," Anya said.

"Magical ability runs in families. It skipped me and my mother, but when I found out I was having a girl I feared the worst. I refused to have my little girl dragged away like Grandma Catherine. Your father agreed and we set about preparing for the worst while hoping the curse would skip another generation."

Another bump rattled Anya as she tried to wrap her mind around what her mother had told her. She found it hard to imagine magic running in her family. Before today she would have sworn they were the most ordinary people in the Empire. She certainly didn't feel like a wizard. What did it feel like to be a wizard? She had no idea.

"Is it really a curse?" Anya asked.

"In the Empire it is." For a moment her mother sounded tired beyond words. Anya wished there was enough light to make out her expression. "Having magical ability is the one certain way to end up a slave of the czar. The White Witches serve as his elite enforcers. They travel the Empire executing his will, crushing anyone that dares speak their mind, when they're not too busy kidnapping girls to make yet more slaves."

"How do you know all this?"

A soft chuckle, almost drowned out by the roar of the engine. "Eighteen years of preparation. I've spoken with many people over that time. We let the resistance use our house as a rest stop on their travels. Since we had you we weren't able to participate in many of the group's more active efforts, but sheltering those in need was something we could do."

"I don't remember seeing any visitors."

"No, there was a secret room in the basement, accessible from a hidden door outside. We did everything possible to keep our mission from you."

"Why? Didn't you trust me?"

"It wasn't a matter of trust." Another sigh in the dark. "You were a child. If you didn't know something you couldn't speak of it. Even an innocent comment to one of your teachers might have meant all our deaths. When you grew up it was already second nature to keep the comings and goings a secret so we kept up the practice. Joining the resistance was our choice, Anya, we didn't want you to suffer for it."

The truck rattled to a stop, cutting her next question off. "What's going on?"

"Shh." Mom shifted and the light from one of the small gaps vanished.

When the light reappeared she whispered, "A checkpoint. Don't make a sound."

Anya's heart thudded so hard she feared that alone might give them away. She held her breath and listened like she'd never listened before.

"State your name and business," a bored voice said.

"Fedor Volkovich, I'm on my way to Mossa to deliver a load of vegetables." After a moment of silence he added, "I come by here twice a week. Don't you ever get tired of this song and dance?"

"It puts food on the table. Can't be fussy at my age. Running kind of late today aren't you, Fedor?" Still bored, but now a hint of curiosity. Anya doubted that was anything they wanted from an official.

"You're telling me. I spent three hours on the side of the road this morning trying to get this piece of junk running again. It'll be a small miracle if I make it home before dark."

A humorless laugh from the official. "I won't keep you then."

A moment later the truck rumbled into motion. Anya peeked out one of the gaps and caught just a glimpse of a man in a white uniform holding a clipboard and making notes.

Beside her Mom groaned. "That was close."

"Won't there be an inspection when we reach Mossa?" Anya asked.

"Yes, but we won't be on the truck when it arrives."

* * *

11

For the next half an hour they bounced along on a slightly less rough road and Anya's mother told her about the resistance and how they became more and more involved. Anya could only shake her head at the secret life her parents led. There was one thing she had to know and while she feared it would be hard for her mother to talk about, she needed to ask.

"How did Dad die?"

"He was killed helping a resistance agent on one of his delivery runs." Mom sniffed and Anya imagined the tears running down her cheeks.

Anya felt around their little compartment until she found her mother's hand and gave it a squeeze. Mom squeezed back and cleared her throat.

"One of the reasons they agreed to help us was because your father took a job at the cannery. The delivery truck gave him a perfect excuse to travel all over the county. They built a compartment to hide people or supplies under the box. He didn't have a package every trip, just now and then. It was bad luck that on the day one of the witches was doing an inspection he was carrying a spy. She found the hidden compartment and killed both your father and the spy."

"Why didn't they come after us?" Anya asked.

"He worked under a false name and when the witch killed him there wasn't..." Mom's voice caught and she was silent for a few seconds. "There wasn't enough left to identify. It isn't unusual for people to disappear, so when your father vanished no one thought much of it. Just another unlucky soul caught up in something the Empire didn't like."

"So what happens now?"

"Now we take the long trail out of the Empire. When we've

escaped you'll be the first wizard to have ever gotten out. Many powerful people will want to talk to us about the Empire. What we know is our bargaining chip. Don't tell them anything until we're safe."

"How long will the trip take?" Anya had studied geography in school of course. The nearest free nation was the Kingdom of the Isles, but how long it would take to get there was another matter altogether.

"If all goes according to plan we should be in London by the middle of August."

"What if things don't go according to plan?"

The truck rattled to a stop. Maybe that was just as well. Anya didn't really want to think about what might happen if they failed.

The truck bed rocked and shifted and a moment later the basket was dragged to one side. Anya squinted against the glare.

"Quickly," Fedor said. "We don't want to be seen on the side of the road."

Anya crawled out and stood up, her legs and back complaining after being cooped up for so long. Her mother climbed out behind her and the three of them hopped down. They'd stopped at the edge of a battered blacktop road. There was no one around for as far as she could see in either direction. She took that as a good sign.

At the edge of the shoulder a clump of evergreen bushes rustled and slipped aside revealing a young man perhaps three years older than Anya. He wore coarse wool pants, a brown jacket, and a fisherman's cap.

Fedor motioned them toward the newly made gap in the shrubbery. Mom took Anya's hand and they hustled down to the stranger. He exchanged a nod with her mother and then they were past. A well-worn trail led away from the road and deeper into the shadowy evergreen forest.

Anya shivered and tried not to think of the stories Dad used to tell about ghosts and wolves that liked nothing better than to eat little girls. She tightened her grip on her bag and tried to peer into the surrounding shadows. They were only stories, nothing to worry about.

Mom stopped and turned toward the road. Fedor passed his keys over to the new guy and joined Anya and her mother on the trail.

"Darko will take the truck the rest of the way." Fedor took the lead and they started down the path. "If they search they will find nothing but a poorly packed load of vegetables."

"Where are we going now?" Anya asked.

"Over the foothills into the next county. Others will be waiting to take us to the train depot. A friend has arranged transport to the port of Anapa."

"And then?" Anya skipped over an exposed root. If she didn't take care she'd break her neck and save the Imperial agents the trouble of executing her.

"A ship across the Black Sea to Constanta."

Anya's eyes nearly bugged out of her head. "We're going through the Land of Night Princes? That's insane. We won't last a night."

Fedor waved a dismissive hand. "The princes hate the czar almost as much as we do. They've been a great ally in our fight. I've spoken to Prince Talon myself and he agreed to grant us safe passage all the way to the German border. In fact, that part of the journey may be the safest leg."

Anya's mind reeled. What did it say about the rest of their journey if traveling a thousand miles through vampire-infested countryside was the safest part?

14

2

INVESTIGATION BEGINS

The house was a burned-up, gutted wreck. A trickle of smoke continued to rise from the remains, tickling the back of Yarik's throat. He wasn't an expert, but even he could tell someone set the blaze. Only a few charred boards remained standing, most of the building having fallen into the basement.

He shook his head, not much to be learned there. Ignoring the charred stink filling the air, he left the boys, two junior agents on a rotation through the county office, to pick through the ruins and turned his attention to the government van parked in the gravel driveway.

A White Witch had signed it out, he hadn't bothered to memorize the woman's name. If you'd met one of the witches, you'd met them all. In fact, Yarik had seen corpses with more variation in personality. If you liked your women arrogant, dismissive, and powerful, you'd love a witch, otherwise, forget it.

He pulled the door open and found a clipboard sitting on

the driver's seat. It held a single piece of paper with a list of names. The first six had an X beside the name. The seventh name was Anya Kazakov, the only daughter of Sasha Kazakov, the registered occupant of this property.

Yarik tossed the clipboard on the seat. Clearly her testing of Miss Kazakov hadn't gone according to plan. Now he was stuck figuring out what went wrong. Damn witches. Nothing but trouble, the lot of them.

"Agent Yarik!" One of his boys—he'd given up trying to learn their names since they'd be gone in six months anyway—stood in the rubble and waved his arms.

Yarik's back popped when he stretched it. He marched over to the edge of the ruined house. "What?"

"We found a skull, sir."

"Anything else?"

He held up a charred length of wood. Even from a distance Yarik could see the crystals set into it. Damn witches.

"Bag the skull and the stick. We've got a dead witch on our hands, boys. We need to find whoever did this and find them fast." If they didn't, they'd have an army of the mad women crawling all over the county making life even more miserable.

Yarik left the boys to finish combing through the house and walked over to his cramped government car. It had been white at some point in its life, every damn thing associated with the government was, but now age and dirt had combined to turn it a sort of yellowish tan. Looked about like what he used to find in his son's diapers.

His throat tightened and he dismissed the memory. Best not to think about Yuri. He'd been dead for twelve years, but try as he might, Yarik still couldn't let go.

Focus on the job, that was the thing to do. He wedged himself behind the wheel and loosened his tie. Whoever had designed the cheap piece of junk hadn't had six-foot-two, three-hundred-pound men in mind.

At least it started on the first try. He pulled out of the drive and turned right up the dirt road. Of all the counties in the Empire, why did a witch have to die in his? There were over a hundred counties and the emperor only knew how many witches, yet he had the horrid luck for this to happen.

He bounced through one of the many ruts and grimaced. If he had to search all the miserable back roads it was going to be a long afternoon.

Twenty miles up the road he reached the nearest check-point. It wasn't much, just two teenagers in white uniforms sitting beside an orange sawhorse. Yarik rolled down his window and dug out his identification.

The blond boy looked at his official seal, then at Yarik's face, then to the seal again. Finally he gathered himself enough to ask, "Can we help you with something, sir?"

"Has Anya Kazakov or her mother come this way?"

"No, sir. We saw smoke." The second guard joined his partner beside Yarik's car. "Was it the Kazakov's place?"

"'Fraid so. You know them?"

"Not personally, sir. Anya was two years behind me at school. I knew her by sight, but we didn't hang out or anything."

"All the boys knew Anya by sight." The second guard gave a wolf whistle. "She's the most beautiful girl in the county."

"Can you give me a description?" Yarik asked more out of curiosity about what they'd say than any need to know. He could call the school and have a picture in five minutes.

The first guard said, "Blond hair, blue eyes, everything else perfect."

The other boy gave an enthusiastic nod. "She's surface-of-the-sun hot."

"Do they have family in the area, somewhere they might go if there was an accident?"

"Not that I know of," Guard One said.

"Okay, keep your eyes open. If you see either of the women, take them into custody. We need to ask them some questions about the fire."

Both boys saluted and returned to their posts. Yarik had seen less inspiring servants of the Empire, but he couldn't recall where. He made a u-turn and drove back down the road. It was fifty miles to the checkpoint in the opposite direction. Fifty miles of pockmarked, rutted, dirt road.

Damn witches.

* * *

Yarik turned off what passed for a main road and onto a secondary road that had just a few less craters than the moon. After striking out at the second checkpoint he only had one option remaining. If Anya and her mother didn't come this way he was flat out of ideas.

As he approached yet another checkpoint, this one manned by a graybeard old enough to be his father, Yarik's radio crackled before a staticky voice said, "We found a hidden room in the basement, sir. It appears the Kazakovs may have been resistance sympathizers. We found no sign of other bodies. What are your orders, sir?"

Yarik stopped and snatched the mic off its holder. "For one thing stop using the radio. If the resistance is involved they monitor government frequencies. When you're finished there take the witch's van to base. I'll be there as soon as I can. Should anything else come up, call my cell."

"Yes, sir."

The radio went quiet and Yarik gave a disgusted shake of his head. Morons. He'd fire the both of them if he could. Unfortunately, they weren't qualified to do anything useful so he was stuck with them, at least for a few more months, then they'd be someone else's problem.

He put the car in gear and eased onto the road. When he reached the checkpoint—this one was literally an old man with a walking stick and clipboard—he stopped and rolled his window down.

The old man hobbled over and looked through the window at him. Yarik flashed his ID. "Has anyone come through here today?"

"Ah, yeh."

A headache was slowly building now. "Who?"

The guard's neck creaked as he turned to look at the clipboard. "Fedor Volkovich. He had a load of vegetables bound for the plant. Fedor's a good boy. Comes through here a couple times a week. Always has a minute to chat. Not today though. Running late. He ought to request a new truck. That piece of junk he's driving is on its last legs. Why I remember back in the ol—"

"What time did he come through?" Yarik asked. Once the old-timers got going you had to be quick or they'd never shut up.

"Twelve forty-seven. I know just what time it was because I checked my watch." The guard dug a silver watch out of his pocket. "I got it when I left the army. Served ten years on the eastern border fighting the Iron Emperor's stone soldiers."

The guard blathered on, but Yarik stopped listening. The

first signs of smoke were called in a little after noon. If Fedor was involved the timing was right.

"You had to use a bazooka to destroy them stone soldiers. I was just a rifleman, never did get to fire one of the rocket launchers. Why I bet—"

"Did Fedor have anyone with him?"

"What? No, course not. Why would he have anyone with him? I told you he had a load of vegetables for the plant."

"Did you search the load?"

"No. I'm just supposed to note the name and time of anyone passing through. No one said anything about searching. If I'm supposed to search someone needs to tell me. I can search alright. Did I tell you about the time—"

"I need to get moving. Good afternoon." Yarik rolled up his window, cutting off the stream of words.

He pulled out around the old man and drove as fast as he dared down the rutted path. The cannery was in Mossa. If he hurried Yarik figured he could make it before shift change.

As he drove he flipped open his phone and hit auto-dial. A moment later a female voice said, "Security Station Fifty-Three, how may I direct your call?"

"Research."

"One moment."

The line went dead and a moment later another voice, this one male, said, "Research."

"Is that you, Rostov?" Yarik asked.

"Agent Yarik. It's been a while since I heard from you. How can I help?"

"I need anything you have on a Fedor Volkovich, especially as it regards a family named Kazakov or the local resistance."

"Got it. This have something to do with the dead witch?"

"Looks like. Call me when you have something. Don't use the radio."

"Understood."

The line went dead and Yarik flipped the phone shut. Rostov was the best researcher in the department. Not that that meant much since they only had two researchers, Rostov and his brother Sergei. Still, if there was something to be found he had confidence Rostov would find it.

An hour later Yarik reached the edge of Mossa. The town consisted of grids of cinderblock apartment buildings, cinderblock shops, a few smaller factories, and the cannery. Two roads ran north and south, one straight to the cannery. At his first real checkpoint of the day, a pair of guards armed with machine guns stood beside a little shack with a gate attached to it. They passed a cigarette back and forth and ignored Yarik. Clearly they didn't recognize his government-issue vehicle.

Yarik rolled down his window and thrust his credentials at them. Fear quickly replaced arrogant indifference. That was the correct reaction when you made a superior wait. Yarik knew plenty of agents that lacked his good nature. His old boss, for instance, would have had these two idiots transferred to the eastern front in a heartbeat if they'd kept him waiting.

The cigarette was quickly stamped out and both guards hurried over. "How can we be of assistance, Agent?" asked the older of the two, a young man with a patchy beard and frayed uniform.

"I'm looking for a Fedor Volkovich. He was headed this way with a load of vegetables for the cannery."

The older guard looked to his companion who trotted over to the guard shack. He reached inside and pulled out a clipboard. He flipped the pages once, nodded, and jogged over to the car. "I found him. Came through just before two. Nothing unusual in my notes."

Yarik nodded and gestured at the gate. The guards hastened to open it for him. When the bar was up he drove through and straight down to the cannery where he stopped at yet another checkpoint. It was a damned wonder they got anything done in the Empire. Everyone was always stopping to talk to guards.

He completed the ritual presentation of identification and a middle-aged man leaned against the hood of his car. "Can I help you, Agent?"

"Fedor Volkovich. He came through at two. Do you remember him?"

The guard shrugged. "We get deliveries all day long. I can't keep track of who's who. As long as they've got vegetables and are on my list, I let them through."

"What time did he leave?"

The guard gave a put-upon groan and stepped into his shack. If the Empire had a stock market, Yarik would have invested in guard shack and uniform makers.

The guard emerged again. "He left fifteen minutes ago. You just missed him."

"What did he look like?"

The guard gazed up at the sky and tapped his chin. "Young lad, mid-twenties maybe. No beard. Had on a funny hat, like sailors wear."

Yarik nodded, snatched his radio mic from its cradle, and switched to the local frequency. "Guard Station One, come in."

A moment of static was followed by a crackly voice. "This is Guard Station One, go ahead."

"This is Agent Yarik. Stop any truck attempting to leave the town. Understood?"

"Yes, Agent. How long do you want us to hold them?"

"Until I've spoken to the drivers. I'm on my way now."

Yarik repeated his message to Guard Station Two and turned towards the edge of town. One of them was bound to catch Fedor. Maybe now he'd get some of his questions answered.

* * *

The guard shack had been reduced to splinters. Empty baskets lay scattered across the road. At least the guards themselves managed to leap aside when the delivery truck refused to stop. They appeared shaken, but no worse for wear. Yarik scrubbed a hand across his face. There was no sign of the truck that had done the running down. Any doubts he'd had about Fedor's involvement with the resistance vanished.

Unfortunately, that meant he was going to have to call regional headquarters. Standing orders were to report all resistance activity at once. No way would he avoid a visit from the witches now.

Why had he decided to join internal security? Yarik asked himself that more and more often as he got older. Not that he had a choice in the matter now. Once you made your career selection that was that. He'd work until he was dead or unable to do the job any longer. That meant another twenty years of this shit, at least.

He groaned, heaved himself out of his undersized car, and ambled over to the trembling guards. They clutched their rifles like they were some sort of magical talisman that would keep them safe.

"Did you get a good look at him?" Yarik asked.

The older guard shook his head. "There was a glare on the windshield, plus I was more focused on the grill about to flatten me. The truck was an old flatbed filled with empty baskets."

"Great, that describes half the trucks in the county. Either of you get off a shot?"

Both men shook their heads. No great surprise there. Neither of them had ever seen any real action, not with a posting in this backwoods county.

He waved them off and went to examine the remains of the shack. Yarik had no idea what he was looking for, inspiration maybe, a portal to some other part of the world. Either would do, but neither seemed likely.

Something wet glinted in the late afternoon light. He bent down and touched it. Dark and a little tacky. Oil maybe, not anti-freeze, not the right color. If the oil pan got busted that was a break for Yarik.

A trail of drops led down the road. If it was oil, the truck wouldn't get far. Maybe he could get a few answers before he had to call headquarters.

"Hey!" When the guards looked his way he waved. "Get in. We're going hunting."

They hustled over with their rifles. "Shouldn't we stay here?" the older guard asked.

"No, this is a priority. Remember, we need Fedor alive." Otherwise he'd have to ask one of the witches to question his corpse. Yarik had been to a necromantic questioning once and the memory still gave him chills.

The guards slid into the back and Yarik got behind the wheel. They had about an hour of daylight left. He took off down the road. With any luck they'd find their man sitting on the shoulder ready to surrender.

Right, and maybe he'd find a sane witch to help him identify the skull.

* * *

The first bullet skipped off the windshield, sending a spiderweb of cracks racing through it. Yarik slammed on the brakes and skidded sideways. Fifty feet up the road a flatbed truck older than he was sat on the shoulder. A second shot smashed into the passenger-side window and blew it to shards.

The younger guard stuck his rifle out the window and opened up on the truck. The acrid stink of cordite filled the car.

The crack of the machine gun nearly deafened Yarik. He drew his service revolver, scrambled out of the car, and eased over to put the engine block between him and whoever was doing the shooting.

When the machine gun finally fell silent Yarik chanced a glance around the front of his car. No one shot at him. On the one hand he was relieved, on the other he feared his overzealous companion may have killed his only lead.

He caught the older guard's eye and pointed at the rear of the car, then he pointed at himself and nodded toward the front. The guard gave him a thumbs up and eased around the trunk.

Yarik broke cover and ran toward the bullet-riddled truck. Still no shots. After the machine gun the silence seemed almost oppressive.

He hopped up on the step and pointed his gun into the cab. Empty, no blood, no Fedor.

"Sir!" the guard said.

Yarik landed on the pavement and ran for the back of the truck. On the opposite side from the road he found the guard standing over a body. A single bullet hole in the side of his head answered one question. The dead man had an automatic pistol in his limp grasp. He'd clearly preferred death to capture. Yarik didn't blame him. He was no more enamored of the witches' interrogation of the living than he was of their questioning of the dead.

"Damn it!" He restrained himself from kicking the corpse by a hair.

"What now, sir?" the guard asked.

"Now you two load this asshole in my car and I take him to headquarters. I might not be able to question him, but the witches can."

An hour later Yarik pulled into the Imperial Security Agency Headquarters and drove around to the rear where a set of steel double doors led to the morgue. A single flickering bulb lit the entrance. He got out, marched up the ramp, and pushed the buzzer.

A moment later a voice asked, "Who is it?"

"Yarik. I need the body haulers out here with a gurney."

"On our way, sir."

Yarik returned to his car and sat on the cooling hood. The day hadn't gone at all well. He accepted that. A good day in the Empire involved keeping your head down, avoiding witches and resistance fighters, and getting home in time to enjoy your wife's dinner.

So far he'd failed on all counts. He checked the time on his phone. Half an hour until dinner. Nope, not tonight. He called to let Iliana know he wouldn't make it while he waited for the body haulers. She wouldn't like it, but at this point his dear wife had resigned herself to his work hours.

"Where are you?" she asked. "The stew's almost ready."

"You'll have to warm it up for me later. I'm going to be late."

His voice must have given something away. "Bad day?"

"Very." The door opened and two big men wearing white coveralls emerged, pushing a gurney with a squeaky wheel. "I have to go. Love you."

"Love you too."

He closed his phone and walked around to watch the haulers load up Fedor. They each grabbed an end and slung him up and out of the trunk. A shallow puddle of blood filled the metal of his trunk. As he stared it slowly drained out a small hole that had rusted through the bottom over the years. He'd get a rookie to hose it out and be good to go in the morning.

"What do you want us to do with the stiff?" one of them asked.

"Cold storage. We'll get a witch to look at him in the morning."

That drew a grunt. The staff didn't like the witches any better than the agents. Yarik followed them inside, taking the first left into the main area of the building. He spotted Rostov working at his desk and went over.

"Find anything?"

Rostov looked up from the computer and peered at Yarik through thick, round glasses. He blinked as though trying to remember what he was supposed to find then finally an invisible light bulb appeared.

"Yes, I put a full report together for you." Rostov shuffled through the stack of files balanced precariously on the edge of his desk and finally yanked one out. "There you are. Everything I could find on Fedor Volkovich."

Yarik accepted the folder. It only had about three pages. "This is it?"

"What can I say? Friend Fedor has lived an exceptionally boring life. Dead wife. No kids. Just work and regular visits to

The Sickle, a cheap bar in Mossa."

Yarik flipped open the file and stared at the picture on the first page. The man had a beard, looked about twenty years older and a hundred pounds heavier than the body he'd just brought in.

"You got the wrong guy," Yarik said.

"I assure you I didn't," Rostov said. "The first page is his official registration downloaded directly from the computer in New St. Petersburg. The picture was updated, along with all his other information, two years ago. That is Fedor Volkovich."

Yarik scowled at the picture. If that was Fedor then who the hell did they have in the fridge?

He returned to his desk and tried to make sense of what he knew. The dead guy was impersonating Fedor. No great challenge there since the various checkpoints only noted the name you provided. They didn't have pictures of every person in the Empire at their fingertips.

The point of the whole exercise eluded Yarik. And for that matter, where were the Kazakov ladies? No one had so much as mentioned either woman and from the sounds of it the daughter at least would draw attention.

He tossed the slender file on his empty desk for later reading and slumped down into the hard plastic chair. What a mess. There was no way around it, he'd have to call for a witch now.

Yarik snatched the handset out of its cradle. No sense putting it off. He dialed the regional command center and after three rings a voice said, "Command center, how can I direct your call?"

"The witch ward," Yarik said.

A moment of silence then, "Hold on."

A beep followed a click. Yarik waited, a little bead of sweat forming on his upper lip. They always made you wait, it was a way of asserting their power.

Finally a cold voice said, "Magic section, what do you need?"

"I have a possibly murdered White Witch on my hands as well as an unidentified body of a young male that was likely involved. I'm requesting a necromantic intervention."

"You're certain the victim is a witch?"

Yarik wouldn't have thought it was possible to get a chill through the phone, but he shivered nonetheless. "I'm as certain as I can be without magical confirmation. Could you get someone here by morning?"

A loud crack was followed by a chill wind swirling through the open space. At the center of the swirling breeze stood a pale woman with white hair, wearing a white robe. It looked like someone had sucked all the color out of the witch. They all looked like that though so he wasn't overly concerned.

"Never mind." Yarik stood and walked over to greet his unwelcome visitor. "Thank you for coming so—"

"Where is my sister's body?" Eyes as hard as diamonds bore into Yarik.

"Burned up, I'm afraid. All we recovered was her skull and the testing device she carried."

"Someone dared burn the body of a White Witch?" The temperature dropped twenty degrees. "Who?"

"We don't know. That's why I called you. I had a lead but he killed himself rather than submit to my questions. The only way we can extract any information now is with magic."

"I will discover who did this. And when I do they'll wish they'd never been born."

Yarik didn't doubt that for a second. It probably wasn't

appropriate, but he found he pitied the poor bastard that killed the witch.

* * *

Yarik walked down the hall toward the morgue, trying his best to ignore the cold radiating in waves off the witch. He'd have icicles hanging off his nose at this rate. A dying light above him flickered and sent crazy shadows dancing around them. How many times had he told maintenance to get that fixed?

Stop trying to distract yourself and focus. He pushed through a set of double doors and into a stainless steel and tile operating room. Beyond a barrier of hanging plastic strips a wall covered in little doors waited.

The body haulers had made themselves scarce, chicken-hearted bastards, so he'd have to handle everything himself.

"Who did you want to see first?"

"My sister." She glared at him as though the answer should have been obvious even to an idiot like him.

And it should have been. The witches only cared for their own and their master, the czar, may he rule forever.

Yarik scanned the rows of doors until he found one that read, *unknown witch*. He opened it and pulled out a steel slab with the bagged skull and charred length of wood resting on it.

The witch approached and Yarik gave her room to work. In fact, he inched as far away as he dared without leaving the room.

She pulled out the blackened skull, ignoring the few scraps of flesh still clinging to it and stared into its empty eye sockets. He had no idea what she hoped to find and he didn't want to know.

A new chill, this one psychic rather than physical, filled the air when she spoke the first word of her spell. Dark energy gathered around the skull, flickering and popping like black lightning. It lifted out of her grasp and hovered at eye level.

She continued to chant and the darkness deepened until Yarik could barely make out the skull itself. When she finally fell silent shadows filled the morgue. Yarik couldn't see the plastic wall or the little metal doors. There was only him, the witch, and the skull. There wasn't another pair in the world he would have less liked to spend his evening with.

"Who killed you, sister?" the witch asked.

The only sound was Yarik's hammering heart. When he began to fear the spell hadn't worked an unearthly voice said, "I don't know."

"Did you see them?"

"No."

Yarik grimaced. So far this was a spectacular failure.

The witch looked his way. "Do you have questions?"

He bit his lip and thought. "Did Anya or her mother do anything to you?"

"No."

That was a relief. Perhaps they had witnessed the murder and ran for it. But in that case he should have found them by now.

"Were you in the house when you were attacked?"

"In the doorway."

"Facing in?"

"Yes."

Yarik nodded and the witch ended her spell. The skull landed on the steel table and the oppressive darkness dissolved.

She stared at him. "You learned something?"

"Yeah, whoever killed your sister moved the body deeper into the house before setting the place on fire. The murderer wanted to be sure the body was destroyed."

"Why?" she asked. "I could have recalled her spirit even without the skull. It only simplified my task."

"Most people aren't that knowledgeable about magic. It's a reasonable precaution for the uninitiated. Unfortunately, we're no closer to figuring out who actually killed your colleague."

"True, but we will find whoever did this, Agent. I promise you no one can get away with killing a White Witch. We won't stand for it and neither will the czar."

Wouldn't want anyone to think you weren't invincible after all. Out loud he said, "I have no doubt we'll find and bring the killer to justice. Perhaps the second body will provide us with more information than your unfortunate sister."

"Perhaps. Show me the body."

Yarik pushed the slab with the witch's skull into its niche and pulled out the one holding the mystery man. The body haulers hadn't bothered to remove his clothes or cover him with a cloth. Even a criminal deserved more dignity than that.

The witch repeated her spell, once more filling the morgue with darkness. Even knowing exactly what was going to happen didn't make Yarik any more comfortable.

She turned to him and said, "Ask your questions."

"Who were you?"

"Darko Donovich." The sepulchral voice seemed to come from everywhere rather than from the dead man's lips.

"Why were you pretending to be Fedor?"

When the spirit didn't answer for half a minute Yarik looked at the witch and raised an eyebrow.

"His spirit resists the spell." She spoke a single, harsh syllable.

A low moan filled the air, a moan of anguish beyond human understanding. When the spirit spoke again its tone sounded even flatter and more emotionless. "Fedor had another mission. I had to complete his delivery."

"What mission?"

"The resistance is helping Anya Kazakov and her mother escape the Empire."

"Why?" the witch asked.

"To show that the czar isn't all powerful and resistance isn't futile. Her escape will prove we have a chance and give others hope."

Her lips twisted in rage, but when she didn't ask any more questions Yarik resumed the interrogation. "What's their plan?"

"To help her escape."

"By what route, what mode of transportation?"

"I don't know. The details were kept from all but those who needed to know." The voice grew softer as it went on.

"Time runs short, Agent," the witch said. "My spell is weakening."

"Where exactly did you last see Anya and what was she doing?"

"Thirty miles south of Mossa on the side of the road. Fedor was to lead the girl and her mother through the forest to the next point on the journey. I took the truck from there to Mossa." The word Mossa became a drawn-out sigh and the oppressive atmosphere vanished.

The witch snapped her fingers and the darkness fled. "That was not so useful."

"On the contrary, we now have a place to start and an idea of what's going on. That's more than I had ten minutes ago. I'll send out an alert to all stations to watch out for our fugitives and first thing in the morning we'll begin the search for wher-ever they left the road. Since they're on foot they won't have too much of a lead on us."

"It had better be as you say. I will be joining your search. My name is Irmina Mercer and the killer of my sister will not escape. I swear it in the czar's name."

Yarik kept his expression neutral, but inside he groaned. Just what he needed, a witch to criticize every move he made.

3

REBELS ON THE RUN

nya wasn't sure she could take another step. For the past she didn't know how many hours she'd been trudging along behind her mother and Fedor. The baked apple felt like a dream from another life, a life that still made some sort of sense. Now she was on the run, and she'd given up asking her mother for more details three hours ago when she discovered she needed all her breath for marching.

The sun hung low in the sky and the trees cast long shadows across the narrow trail. Roots and loose rock hid, waiting to send her sprawling on her face. So far she'd avoided an embarrassing spill, but Anya was no outdoorswoman. She didn't like bugs or dirt or camping and she was getting to despise hiking. If they had to walk all the way to the train yard she might take her chances with the witches.

Or at least she might have if Fedor hadn't killed the one that came for her. If they got their hands on her now, Anya doubted she'd receive gentle treatment. No, whatever came of this mad plan, she had no choice but to see it through.

Five minutes later faint sounds filled the air. It sounded like voices, but who in the world would be out in the middle of the forest?

She found out a moment later when they rounded a bend and the trail opened up into a clearing. A handful of fires burned and the scent of roasting meat set her mouth to watering. She hadn't eaten anything since breakfast and found she was starving.

"What is this?" she asked.

"A resistance camp," Fedor said. "We'll be picking up some help before we continue our journey in the morning. You two must be hungry. We'll eat and then perhaps we can answer your many questions."

Getting answers seemed a good deal less important at the moment than eating. Fedor led them into the clearing. A young man in gray carrying a machine gun approached and after a few words motioned them through.

They went to the nearest fire. A woman tended a bubbling pot, stirring it with a wooden spoon. Anya stared for a moment. She hadn't expected to find women mixed in with the rebels. Though why it should surprise her she didn't know. Her own mother had gotten involved with the group after all.

The cook offered a gap-tooth smile and ladled up a bowl of stew for her. Anya accepted it along with a bent spoon and set to eating. The gravy had a mild spice she didn't recognize and the meat fell apart when she cut it. After hours of hiking it tasted like the finest meal in the world.

She'd emptied half the bowl before Anya realized she hadn't thanked the woman. "This is delicious. Thank you."

"You're welcome, dear."

Anya glanced at her mother and found she was engrossed

in conversation with one of the rebels. Probably someone she'd met at the house.

Anya returned her attention to the cook. "I didn't expect to find women with the group. Do you mind if I ask why you joined the resistance?"

The cook's gentle expression turned hard and for a moment Anya feared she'd said something she shouldn't have. The grim look lasted only a moment then a sigh blew it away.

"I joined because my daughter was like you, a wizard candidate. The witches took her from me and I haven't seen her since. That was five years ago and god only knows where she is and what they've done to her. When I heard of the mission to help you escape I volunteered at once. If I can save you..." the woman sniffed and looked away.

Anya wasn't sure what to say so she returned to her meal. Try as she might, Anya couldn't imagine life anywhere else. All she'd ever known was the Empire and their little house, an equally small school, and her few friends. It wasn't a perfect life, but until today she'd been fairly content.

Anya cleaned her bowl and yawned. Desire for sleep warred with her need to know exactly what was going on. Mom finished her discussion and turned to face her. It looked like answers would be the winner. Fedor shifted, completing their little semicircle.

"You wished to know more of our plans," he said. "Here they are. We mean to smuggle you out of the Empire, across Europe, to the Kingdom of the Isle. We've spent ten years laying plans and preparing for this moment."

Anya stared, stunned by what he said. Ten years the resistance had been planning this? All she knew about the place was what she learned in school. The teachers said they were a weak, decadent nation that allowed their people to decide who represented them and let their wizards run free. It didn't seem so bad to her, especially now that she was one of those wizards.

"Why now? Why me?" she asked.

"Our contacts in the Kingdom requested we bring out a wizard," Fedor said. "They're curious about how powerful you are without the czar's curse twisting your magic, their words not mine. Of course, we didn't know until today that you would be the one we brought out. Sasha volunteered to leave with us if you passed the test. When you did, things happened quickly."

"So what next?"

"In the morning we set out for Dorcha where we'll hop a train to Anapa. That'll take at least ten days."

"I can't believe they'd go out of their way just to meet an uncorrupted witch."

Fedor barked a laugh. "Hardly. We've prepared documents that reveal everything we know about the Empire. You're just the icing on the cake. Your presence tipped the scales in our direction."

Her head spun. It was all too much. Anya looked to her mother who had a sad smile.

"I refuse to let them have you," she said.

Anya nodded, curled up in a little ball, and hoped everything made more sense in the morning.

* * *

The dawn light revealed a most welcome sight to Anya: four crudely built dune buggies. They looked like piles of scrap someone bolted wheels to, but they had engines so at least she wasn't going to have to hike all the way to Dorcha.

She sat up and groaned. Sleeping on the ground hadn't done her back or neck any good.

She got to her feet and her spine popped. Her mouth tasted like a family of mice had moved in, but there didn't appear to be anywhere to get washed up or brush her teeth. A quick glance around the clearing revealed the rebels in all their dubious glory.

Eleven men and women dressed in tattered clothes crouched around last night's fire pits. The men had scruffy beards and the women's hair was a tangled mess. She reached up and found her own hair in a similar state. They'd seemed more impressive last night, sitting in the dark, tending their fires. In the harsh light of day it became clear that they were desperate, ragged people straddling the line between survival and starvation. At least they all had guns.

The sight did little to fill her with confidence. On the other hand, they didn't look like they had much to lose, so maybe that would motivate them to overcome their circumstances. For her and her mother's sake she certainly hoped so.

"Good morning, kiska."

She'd been so wrapped up in her thoughts Anya hadn't even noticed her mother approach. A familiar hand squeezed her shoulders and she reached up and squeezed back. At least Mom was here. That fact made her feel better than it probably should have.

"Hi, Mom. Did you sleep?"

"A little." Gentle pressure brought Anya around to face her. In her free hand Mom held a biscuit studded with cheese. "Breakfast?"

Anya accepted the food and bit down. Flakey goodness filled her mouth and brought a happy groan. Nothing like hunger to make the food taste delicious. All around her people were packing and scattering the remains of the fires. It wouldn't do much to hide the fact that they'd camped here, but every little bit helped.

She sighed and finished her meal. How did they make something so tasty out here?

Her mother held out a blue leather booklet. "This is your new identity. Memorize it and burn the one you brought from home. The only thing worse than getting caught with false documents would be getting caught with both new and old papers."

Anya flipped open the booklet. Anya Ventorova. At least they let her keep her first name. Probably a good idea lest she forget to answer to a new one. Anya was common enough that it shouldn't draw a second look.

She dug her old book out of her bag, found a still-burning fire, and tossed it in. Just like their house, it went up in flames. No going back now.

Half an hour later they were roaring down a rough road cut through the pines by heavy equipment years ago. Anya sat beside Fedor who drove the best of the dune buggies, a four-seater with a proper roll cage. On the back seat her mother and another man she didn't know crowded together. Not the most comfortable arrangement, but it beat walking.

"When can I drive?" Anya shouted over the roar of the engine.

Fedor shot her a dubious look, but didn't refuse outright. Not that she expected him to give in easily. This wasn't a pleasure trip after all.

They traveled over the rough paths all morning until a little after noon when Fedor slowed. They rounded a bend and found a shack not much bigger than an outhouse, built of rough logs, moss, and vines.

The dune buggies came to a stop beside the shack and Anya jumped out. Her legs almost gave out after hours of sitting in the cramped seat. She looked left and right, her knees locked together.

A gentle tap on the shoulder got her to turn around. The woman that cooked for her the night before had left her transport and come over.

"You'll have to use the bushes, dear, no bathrooms out here."

Anya grimaced, but ran over behind a clump of low bushes. When she finished she returned to the group in time to see Fedor emerge from the shack. He was scowling and his fists clenched and relaxed like he wanted to strangle someone.

The rest of the group busied themselves filling the buggies from bright-red gas cans. Anya reached her mother at the same time Fedor did. Two of the others joined them. No one had introduced themselves to her and she figured that was intentional. She couldn't tell what she didn't know after all.

"Bad news?" Mom asked.

"Darko didn't make the rendezvous last night. Our mole says a witch arrived early yesterday evening. We have to assume they know our plans."

"How much did Darko know?" Mom asked.

"No details, just that we planned to smuggle the two of you out of the Empire. That's still enough to cause us trouble. They'll have lookouts posted on all the roads. That shouldn't be a big deal since we're traveling cross country, but when we reach Dorcha things could get dicey."

"Let's not borrow trouble," Mom said. "We're days from reaching the city. Plenty might still go wrong between here and there."

Fedor grunted. "True enough. Load up. We've got a long ways to go."

* * *

Yarik stood, arms crossed, and surveyed the clearing. Six cold fire pits, matted down hay—a large group had camped there for several nights. They were long gone now, but it seemed clear that this was where the true Fedor had led Anya and her mother. They were still a step behind and Yarik hated being behind.

Noon had come and gone an hour ago. If only they'd managed to find the path sooner. He shook his head at the useless wish. His men had done their best and he couldn't ask for more than that.

His stomach grumbled and he pulled out one of the peanut butter crackers he'd grabbed from the vending machine before they left. He'd barely popped it in his mouth when one of his men shouted, "Sir! We found something."

Chewing as he ambled over, Yarik tried to put himself in the rebels' minds. How would he try to get Anya out of the Empire? Certainly none of the obvious methods would work, not now that the security service had caught their scent.

Near the edge of the clearing were four separate tracks leading west. They were too close together to be car tracks so that meant ATVs of some sort.

Shit!

They'd never catch up on foot and the agency didn't have anything usable of their own, at least not within a day's travel and by the time something arrived it would be too late. They'd have to circle around and hope to pick the rebels up on the far side of the forest.

"Agent Yarik." Irmina strode up, a harsh frown creasing her pale features. "What's the problem?"

"Our targets have acquired transportation. No way we can keep up on foot."

"Perhaps you can't." She chanted in one of the wizards' nonsense languages and when she stopped she floated a foot off the ground. "But I can."

She turned east.

"Wait!" Irmina glared at him. "Do you have a phone or radio or something we can use to keep in touch?"

"A White Witch has no need of such mundane things."

No, of course they didn't. However, Yarik didn't want to end up with another dead witch on his hands. It would look bad on his record not to mention his boss might have him shot.

"Igor!" Yarik said.

A stout twenty-two-year-old agent in a stained gray suit huffed and puffed his way over. "Sir?"

"Mistress Irmina needs to borrow your phone. Be a good lad and dig it out."

Igor pulled a blocky little flip phone from his inner pocket and held it toward the witch like he feared she might take his hand along with the phone.

Irmina glared at both of them and for a minute he feared she might refuse. Finally, she snatched the phone out of Igor's hand. Fedor sighed in relief.

"I will contact you when I've captured them." Irmina tucked the phone into her white robes and flew away after the tracks.

Yarik waited until she was out of sight then groaned. This was why he hated working with witches. They all wanted to go off and do their own thing. Not a team player in the bunch.

"Round up the boys, Igor. We're going back to the cars."

"Do you think she'll be able to capture the whole group on her own?" Igor asked.

"No, I suspect she'll kill most of them and capture the leaders, hopefully near an access road. I don't know about you, but I've had enough hiking for one day."

Igor broke into a smile revealing a broken front tooth. "I'm with you there, sir."

He saluted and went to collect the rest of the team. Yarik sighed. It was important to keep up the boys' morale. Having a witch around wore them out. Now all he needed was someone to lift his morale and he'd be all set.

* * *

Anya wasn't sure if it was the steady vibration of the engine, the noxious fumes coming out of the exhaust, or the fact that she didn't sleep worth a damn the night before, but she found herself half dozing off as they roared through the forest. She blinked and yawned, trying to shake it off. Their little group had left the shack three hours ago and were now in the middle of god knew where.

"Witch!" The shouted warning came from one of the other buggies.

A burst of adrenaline washed away her weariness in an instant. She twisted around, but saw nothing. Where was she?

A blast of lightning sent dirt flying between Anya's buggy and the one to her right. She tried to track where the attack had come from. For an instant she thought she saw a ghost of white flitting between the trunks, but it vanished before she could say for sure.

Two of the buggies skidded to a stop. The rebels on board scrambled out and drew their weapons.

"What are they doing?" Anya shouted as Fedor hit the accelerator. Seven people with guns were no match for a White Witch.

"Buying us time."

Another crack shattered the air and a pine tree came crashing down in front of them.

Fedor barely slammed on the brakes in time to avoid crashing into the trunk. The pine tree had to be a foot and a half in diameter and it blocked the whole road. It seemed the witch didn't intend to let them escape.

The shifting lever clunked into reverse and Fedor backed up to join those who'd remained behind. A man in black carrying an old bolt-action rifle ran over. "What are you doing?"

"We have to use it," Fedor said "She blocked the road."

"If we use it now we'll be defenseless and it's a long way to the border."

Anya didn't know what they planned to use, but they'd better do it fast. A flutter of white drew her attention to the sky. The witch descended and hovered a few feet from the gathered rebels.

"Surrender now and your deaths will be quick," she said.

The woman from the cook fire raised her pistol and fired. A gust of wind roared and blew the bullet aside.

As if it was a signal all the rebels opened fire.

What looked like a tornado sprang up around the witch.

When the guns fell silent the winds died, revealing their unharmed opponent. The witch favored them with a sneer of contempt.

"Pathetic." She gestured and the winds grabbed the woman that fired first, lifted her up and slammed her into a roadside tree twenty feet up. She hung there, impaled by three branches. The witch watched her bleed, a little smile on her cruel face.

Fedor pulled a black crystal the size of a hen's egg out of his pocket. The man that had objected earlier nodded.

Fedor drew back and hurled the crystal at the witch. The wind flared up again, but the crystal punched through it.

The witch's eyes widened a moment before the gem crashed into her chest.

It shattered.

Magic flared, forcing Anya to look away.

When she looked back a seven-foot-tall black crystal floated where the witch had been a moment before.

* * *

Yarik was three hours into a five-hour cross-county trip and enjoying his time away from the witch when his phone rang. Who could that be? The guys in the car behind couldn't need anything and he wasn't expecting to hear from anyone at headquarters.

He grimaced and groped through his pockets for three rings before finally getting a grip on his little phone. It would have been nice if the cheap piece of junk had caller ID, but since the government provided it he only had the most basic features.

He flipped it open. "Yarik."

"I require your presence at once," Irmina said.

Yarik held the phone away from his ear and stared at it as though it had betrayed him. "I'm on the road. We should reach the far side of the forest in two hours. Where are you?"

"In the forest. I'm not exactly sure where. The rebels had a magical artifact. They used it to trap me and escape."

Yarik smothered a laugh. If she heard him he'd be dead the instant they met up. "Okay, we should be able to track your cellphone signal so be sure not to turn it off. We'll be there as soon as we can."

"Hurry, Agent. While you dawdle the enemy escapes."

The line went dead and he tossed the phone into the passenger seat. Arrogant bitch, blaming him for the targets' escape when she was the one they captured. Probably got over-confident and let them get the drop on her. Served her right. Maybe she'd be more careful next time.

Yarik grabbed his radio mic. "Guys, pull over a second. Igor, we have the cellphone tracker, right?"

If they didn't, he'd have to go to the local base at Dorcha and borrow one. That would take an extra couple hours which would do nothing to improve the witch's mood.

The radio crackled and Igor said, "Yes, sir, in the trunk. Why?"

Yarik pulled off the side of the road and switched on his hazard lights. "Just get it out. We need to find Irmina."

Igor pulled in behind him and everyone got out. From the trunk Igor removed a box with a hand-held antenna. He flipped the power switch, punched in a series of numbers, and spun in a slow circle. Yarik didn't know how his subordinate managed so well with technology, but he had the knack.

When he paused Igor faced the forest and a little bit back the way they'd come. "That way, maybe forty or fifty miles."

Yarik stared at the sprawling expanse of evergreens. How in the world would he reach her through all that? There had to be logging roads, that was what the resistance was using to move around. If she confronted them it had to be on or near one of the roads.

He frowned at his pitiful car. No way could he take that through the woods. Yarik tapped his chin and tried to think.

"Are there any logging operations in the area?" Yarik asked.

All he got in answer were blank stares. Why should he be surprised? It wasn't security agency business so his men would have no reason to know about it.

Yarik retrieved his phone and dialed base. "Rostov? I need you to check the county records and find me the nearest logging operation."

"Should I ask why you want to find loggers when you're supposed to be looking for rebels?"

"No."

"Hold on." Yarik barely heard the clicking of Rostov's keyboard. "Okay, I've got three registered jobs. Where are you?"

"Eighty miles east of Dorcha on Seven E."

"Ugh! You're thirty miles from the nearest location." Rostov rattled off a series of directions. "Did you get all that?"

"More or less. If I get lost I'll call again." Yarik hung up. "Load up, boys. We're going hunting."

* * *

Anya had never been to Dorcha before. The caravan of dune buggies stopped at the edge of the forest on a hill overlooking the city. Even from a distance it looked grungy and rough. Smokestacks chugged black smoke into the air which mingled with the exhaust from the train depot to stain the whole city gray. Like everything else in the Empire, the squatty buildings were constructed of cinderblocks and concrete with metal roofs. If there existed a more dingy place in the world she couldn't imagine it.

Anya, her mother, and Fedor got out of their buggy and one of the remaining rebels climbed behind the wheel. Fedor exchanged a few quiet words and the group took off. Anya watched them until they were out of sight. Her chest felt tight and her breath came in ragged gasps. They were on their own again. Somehow having a larger group felt safer, though after the encounter with the witch she realized the stupidity of that idea.

Fedor checked his watch. "We need to get going. Our train is supposed to leave in three hours."

"What about the others?" Anya asked. "Will they be okay?"

Fedor started down a narrow path toward the city. "I hope so. Their job now is to lay a false trail that will hopefully buy us the time we need."

Anya and her mother fell in behind him. "What was that thing you used to stop the witch?"

"A gift from one of our allies. If all goes according to plan you'll meet Lord Talon in three weeks."

"But what was it?"

"I have no idea. He said if I ever found myself in an encounter with a witch with no hope of escaping to throw it at her."

"Not the most detailed instructions," Mom said.

Fedor barked a laugh. "No, but it worked and that's what matters."

The path brought them to a wheat field. The golden stalks came up to Anya's chest. The field spread as far as she could see in either direction. At the far end a road waited to take them into the city.

"Won't we have to go through a checkpoint?" Anya asked.

"Yes, a very specific one. We have a friend waiting. Keep low." Fedor crouched down and set out through the grain.

Mom motioned her to go first so she bent low and followed Fedor's tracks. For a time her world became a golden forest of tiny stalks. A small part of her, the part that wanted to pretend she was still a regular girl and all she had to worry about was taking the career placement exam, tried to pretend this was all a game of hide and seek. And it was, except the people doing the seeking wanted to kill them.

Half an hour later they stopped at the edge of the field. Cars and trucks whizzed by on the nearby road. There wasn't a bit of foot traffic to be seen.

When Anya mentioned it Fedor said, "Don't worry, plenty of locals walk into town. There's a footpath half a mile to the south that leads to our inside man's post. You know, we've been planning this for years. Have a little faith."

Anya had plenty of fear, anxiety, and anger, but she was low on faith. Maybe if they made it to the train without any witches appearing she'd dredge some up.

Once more Fedor led the way, this time skirting the road and hurrying along at the edge of the field. Just as he'd said they reached the end of the field and found a footpath that ran parallel to the street. They stepped out and started toward the city.

Anya clenched her bag tighter as they approached one of the innumerable guard shacks that dotted the country. She'd heard you couldn't travel more than a hundred miles in any direction without running into one.

Ahead of them a man and woman reached the shack. Three men in white uniforms emerged and a brief conversation ensued. Documents were examined and they were allowed in. Nothing to it, as long as you weren't a wanted woman.

Fedor slowed his pace to a crawl.

"What's wrong?" Mom asked.

"There were only supposed to be two guards, our friend and a lazy sergeant that made him do all the work."

"What does that mean for us?" her mother asked.

Anya wondered the same thing, but couldn't force the words through her clenched teeth.

"I don't know." Fedor's doubt sent a shudder through her. This was it. They were going to die before even escaping the county. "We'll just have to go through with it and hope our friend has a plan."

Hope someone they'd never met could solve their problem for them. That was the plan? It took every ounce of courage she could muster to keep putting one foot in front of the other. What choice did she have? It wasn't like she had anywhere to run.

When they were three hundred yards away Fedor said, "Remember, we're just regular folks visiting family in the city. Don't do anything to make them more suspicious than they already are. Take your new documents out now so you'll be ready."

Anya dug the little booklet out of her pocket and forced herself not to squeeze it too tight. She didn't want to tear the stupid thing.

Another person, a woman on her own, went through the checkpoint then it was their turn. Anya took a deep breath and forced herself to relax. Her nerves would be more likely to get them caught than anything.

"Papers." She looked up at the gaunt face of a middle-aged officer wearing a crisp white uniform. He held out a gloved hand and Fedor put his false documents into it.

The guard pursed thin, bloodless lips as he studied the forgery. Beside him a fat slob in a stained uniform watched the proceeding with supreme disinterest. A third, younger man stood behind his superiors, his gaze darting from the head guard to Fedor and back again. He had to be the inside man. He didn't look like the sort of person you'd want to rely on to get you out of trouble. The poor guy looked as nervous as Anya felt.

Finally the guard handed Fedor his papers and turned to Mom. She handed him her booklet and even smiled. Anya doubted she'd have had it in her. Her mother was tougher than she'd thought.

The guard gave Mom her papers and turned his cold, blue eyes on Anya. He held out his hand a third time and she handed her ever-so-slightly trembling booklet to him. He snatched it and started reading. After a heart-stopping minute he handed them back.

"Everything appears in order," he said.

Her heart soared. They'd done it. The fake documents had gotten them through.

"There's just one more thing." He reached into the shack and emerged with a testing stick like the witch brought to their house. He offered it to Anya. "All girls appearing to be between the ages of fifteen and twenty must be tested. There's a missing wizard candidate you see and we can't take any chances."

She reached for it, knowing exactly what was going to happen. They were doomed. She'd been stupid to think they could escape. The Empire was too vast and powerful.

Her fingers brushed the wood and the first gem lit up.

The guard's lip curled in a vicious smile. "Ms. Kazakov. We've been looking everywhere for you. The czar is eager to make your acquaintance."

* * *

Yarik swore to himself that he'd never complain about the roads being rough again. Their commandeered skidder, a rusty beast of a machine with tires taller than Yarik and designed to drag logs out of the woods, bounced along the four-foot-deep ruts, jarring his insides, and reminding him once more why he hated witches. At least the sun was out and the fresh-cut pine smelled nice—the little of it that reached him over the diesel exhaust anyway.

To say that the loggers hadn't been thrilled when a group of security agents rolled up on their job site and demanded a ride into the woods would have been understating things by a fair bit. The five rugged men might have been annoyed, but they weren't stupid. Beyond a few grumbles they quickly complied with his orders.

Seated on the opposite fender Igor had his eyes locked on the screen of his tracking device. Yarik had ordered the rest of the team to remain with the cars. He doubted Irmina would appreciate having every man under his command watching her rescue.

They came to an intersection of roads and Igor pointed left. The huge machine lurched, forcing Yarik to tighten his grip.

"We're close!" Igor shouted over the roar of the engine. They rumbled along for another minute. "A quarter mile!"

Yarik tapped the operator on the shoulder and drew his finger across his throat. The driver shifted into neutral and switched the machine off.

"Wait here," Yarik said. "We'll be back soon."

The logger shrugged. "If I don't make my quota this week I'm blaming you."

"You think that'll help?"

His comment brought a humorless laugh. "I don't expect it would."

Yarik patted his shoulder. "Don't worry. I'll leave a requisition letter for half a day's work. As long as you're not off by more than that, you'll be fine."

The logger raised an eyebrow. "That's decent of you."

He didn't add, "for a government agent" but Yarik heard it all the same. He wasn't surprised. Most of his comrades in the security forces enjoyed using their authority to force others to do what they wanted even as they resented their own superiors doing it to them. Petty tyrants and bullies, every son of a bitch in the government.

Yarik despised most of them, but he had to put food on the table so he kept his mouth shut and did his job. He slid to the ground, grateful to be off his uncomfortable seat. After a couple awkward steps he joined Igor in front of the skidder.

"Lead on." Yarik motioned his second ahead of him.

Igor shuffled along, his gaze darting between the tracker and the rough ground. It was slow going, but when they rounded a clump of short evergreens they found a seven-foot-tall black crystal floating a foot off the ground.

Yarik rubbed his eyes. Had he breathed in too many fumes? "You see that thing too, right?"

Igor nodded, his mouth partway open.

Yarik dug out his phone and dialed.

She answered it on the first ring. "What's taking you so long?"

"We're here," Yarik said. "How do I get you out?"

"The crystal is only immune to magic. Hit it with something heavy and it'll shatter."

"Understood." He hung up and looked around for a good-sized rock. It didn't take long to find one that fit in his hand. "Move away a little, just in case."

He didn't have to tell Igor twice. His subordinate scrambled back a hundred feet.

Yarik cocked his arm and slammed the rock into the crystal. A spiderweb of cracks ran through it. One more ought to do it.

He drew back and gave it another rap. The trap fell apart, but instead of pieces of crystal falling to the ground, they dissolved and vanished into the air.

Irmina landed on the ground and stumbled. Yarik reached out without thinking and steadied her. The witch glared and yanked her arm out of his grasp. Typical.

"Are you well?" he asked.

"Fine. The magic doesn't prevent air from entering. Lucky for me considering how long it took you to get me out."

Yarik choked on several retorts. "Sorry. We should get to Dorcha as soon as possible."

"I'll be there in half an hour. Join me as soon as you can." The witch chanted and streaked up into the air.

Yarik watched until she was just a speck in the sky. "You're welcome."

4
RACE TO THE TRAIN STATION

Anya couldn't stop staring at the guard's gaunt face. It had never occurred to her that they might have a testing device. She'd assumed only witches carried them.

A sharp chuff sounded and something wet splattered her face. The guard collapsed as a red stain spread across his fine uniform. A second chuff and the fat guard collapsed, revealing the young man holding a small pistol with a long cylinder attached to the barrel.

Fedor grabbed the pistol and punched the spy in the face. He went down in a heap among the corpses.

"Quickly," he said. "Someone will surely report the shots."

He grabbed the still-stunned Anya and hustled her through the gate and into the city. Her mother brought up the rear. She seemed awfully calm considering they'd just witnessed two men get murdered.

Anya barely registered the drab buildings as they hurried along. Mom stayed on one side of her and Fedor the other, shielding her from the other pedestrians' view. She tried to think, but her mind refused to obey.

A minute or two later they entered a low building. The smell of cooking food turned her stomach and it took all her will not to throw up. Mom gently grasped her by the arm and guided her into a nearby bathroom.

She led Anya to the sink and turned the water on. While it heated up Mom went to the towel dispenser. Anya stared at herself in the mirror. Blood covered her face and dress. She looked like a madwoman from a horror movie.

Her hands shook so bad when she reached up to wipe the blood away she feared she might poke her eyes out. Mom returned, towels in hand, and washed her face like she'd done when Anya was still a little girl.

"We're safe now, kiska." Mom spoke in a soft, reassuring voice. "Let's get you cleaned up."

When her face and hands were clean, Anya stripped off the bloodstained dress and slipped into her spare, a loose, pale-blue sundress. She liked to wear it during the far too brief summers.

"There," Mom said. "Don't you look pretty. Do you feel better?"

"I just saw two people killed before my eyes, we burned our house down, and now we're racing to a future I can't imagine in a country I've only read about in books. So no, I am far, far away from better."

"I'm sorry this happened to you, kiska. Sometimes in life we just get dealt a bad hand. But I promise, I promise, life will be better in the Kingdom of the Isles than it ever could be here. We'll be free. There'll be no checkpoints, no security agents, and best of all, no White Witches. You'll have the chance to use your gift as you want to use it, or to not use it at all. The important thing is that it will be up to you."

Anya tried to imagine the life her mother described, but it wouldn't come. The ideas were too foreign. She took a deep breath to steady herself. "So what now?"

"Fedor is speaking to our contact upstairs. Assuming everything is ready we'll head for the train depot to catch our ride out of here."

"Won't the security people on the train spot us?"

Mom looked away. "We're not traveling by passenger train."

Anya frowned. "How then?"

"I believe our car is carrying furniture. At least we'll have somewhere to sit."

"Great. I guess it could be worse." An image of the dead men popped into her head. Yes, it could certainly be worse.

* * *

Fedor watched a moment as Sasha led her trembling, blood-soaked daughter toward the bathroom. He doubted anyone could see the mess in the dark bar which was just as well. Not that anyone here would say anything. The Black Hammer bar and grill was a rebel hangout and Imperials got a cold welcome and quick kick in the ass back out.

He sighed as the ladies disappeared into the bathroom. Anya was a strong girl, stronger than he had any reason to hope for. Though shaken, she hadn't frozen up, thank god for that. If she'd started screaming or fainted, they'd have been in real trouble. With a final shake of his head Fedor made his way toward the bar.

A young woman with six studs in her nose leaned over and smiled at him. "What can I get you?"

"A Fizzy Dragon."

Her smile vanished as quickly as it appeared. "Behind the bar, up the steps, first door on your right."

Fedor nodded and hopped over the bar. A narrow door led to the kitchen where three people in white chef's coats were busy cooking at a long grill. They never so much as glanced his way so Fedor ignored them and climbed the spiral staircase to his left. It was a narrow fit for a man his size, but he made it up to the second floor.

He turned right and rapped on the closed door. "Come in."

Fedor pushed the door open and stepped inside a simple office filled with papers, binders, a copy machine that looked like it came from the Elf War, and a desk with a slim man in a dark suit behind it. The man rose and held out his hand. "Fedor, you're a little behind schedule."

Fedor took the fine-boned hand in his blunt paw. "We ran into a few difficulties. You're The Manager?"

"Correct. Tell me everything."

Fedor did as he asked and when he finished The Manager said, "Running into a witch so early was unfortunate, but you handled matters well. I'm confident we made the right choice in agreeing to let you escort the young lady on her journey."

"Thank you, sir."

"A general alert has gone out to all security forces along with your descriptions. That was expected and shouldn't be a problem. Our spy says three witches have been assigned to the search. Avoiding them is our biggest priority."

"When do we move?"

"Immediately. I've arranged transport to the train station. The truck will arrive in five minutes. Don't worry about the guard, I'm sure young Karis will be fine. That boy's been a fine undercover asset. He's quick on his feet and knows when to keep his mouth shut."

The Manager came around the desk and went over to the right-hand wall. He tapped twice and a secret panel opened. From within he pulled a worn duffle bag. "Everything you'll need for the train ride you'll find inside."

Fedor took the bag and unzipped it. It wasn't that he didn't trust The Manager, but he liked to know what he had to work with. Inside were ration packs, two automatic pistols and ammunition, a change of clothes for each of them, and a first aid kit. Minimal, but as long as they didn't run into any major issues it should suffice.

He zipped the bag up. "If there's nothing else, sir, I should collect Sasha and Anya."

"No, there's nothing more I can do for you. I'll call the truck and have them meet you at the loading dock. Good luck."

"Thank you, sir." Fedor turned and left the office. The Manager had done all he could. It was up to them now.

* * *

The late afternoon sun hung low in the sky when Yarik finally reached Dorcha. The limited light hid some of the dingy grayness of the city, but it didn't help much. Did the Imperial designers lay out the cities like this in the hope of depressing the populace so they wouldn't think of joining the rebellion? Probably not since the cities predated the rebels by centuries.

Yarik sighed. He'd planned to arrive for lunch and be home for a late dinner, but thanks to the witch it looked like he'd be spending the night. As he approached the eastern checkpoint Yarik frowned. A large group of white-clad security officers had gathered around the guard shack that serviced the pedestrian entrance. What in the world could have happened to warrant that many officers?

His turn came. He rolled down his window and pulled out his identification. One look and the gate guard saluted and raised the bar for him.

Before Yarik pulled through he asked, "What happened next door?"

"Horrible thing, sir. A rebel attack. Two guards were murdered and a third injured. They're trying to get things sorted out now."

"Did a White Witch named Irmina come through here?"

The guard chuckled. "The witches don't come through the gates, sir. They fly straight to the Dragon Temple in the city center."

Yarik nodded. "Thanks."

The guard blinked in astonishment. Yarik drove through and immediately hooked a left over to the foot entrance. He found a parking place a hundred yards up the street and got out. Igor and the boys joined him a moment later.

"What's happening, sir?" Igor asked.

"Resistance activity. If there's any chance it has something to do with our targets we need to check it out."

"What about the witch?"

Yarik shrugged. Irmina was doing her own thing, the way witches always did. He couldn't worry about her if he wanted to catch his missing family. "She's probably at the Dragon Temple. If you want to go check in with her, I don't mind."

"No, sir," Igor said. "We'll stick with you."

That drew quick nods of agreement from the junior agents, just as Yarik knew it would. He doubted they'd even let a junior agent into the temple. They'd probably just turn them into rats and feed them to the cats that hung out all over the place.

He smiled to himself at the idea of Igor as a rat and strolled over to the scene. Yarik had his ID out as he approached and a city officer waved him through. One good thing about being an Imperial security agent was that his authority extended to every corner of the Empire and he outranked all but the highest city officials.

Yarik spotted an officer with a gold badge on his chest marking him as the highest-ranking individual present. He walked over and when the officer noticed him asked, "What happened?"

"Who are you and who let you into my crime scene?" the officer asked.

"Senior Security Agent Yarik Borodinov. That young man back there let me through."

The officer's Adam's apple worked as he tried to swallow. "I'm terribly sorry, Agent. It's this horrible situation. It's got me on edge."

"Perfectly understandable. You were saying?"

"Yes, sir. It appears one or more resistance fighters attacked the checkpoint and broke through into the city. I have men trying to locate them now, but I fear they'll simply blend into the populace. The bastards have a knack for it."

"Indeed. So you have no description and no real idea of numbers, is that correct?"

The officer blanched. "I'm afraid so, sir. Our only survivor was attacked from behind and rendered unconscious before his comrades were killed. To take three of our guards so completely by surprise, I assume more than one assailant was involved."

"A reasonable assumption. Where is your survivor? I'd like to speak with him and offer a commendation for his survival."

That brightened the gloomy fellow's expression. Commendations for a subordinate made the commander look good too. "Right this way, sir."

Yarik followed his guide off to the right out of sight of the crime scene. Seated on a stretcher was a young man in his mid-twenties with sandy hair and a very broken nose. He held his head in both hands, the very image of a soldier grieving his fallen comrades.

"Guard Karis, on your feet!" the officer said.

Karis's head snapped up and he winced before lurching halfway off the stretcher.

"That's alright, son. No need to stand on protocol after all you've been through. Just relax."

Karis slumped down and the officer —Yarik really should ask the man his name, but he just couldn't muster the interest — stared at him like he'd grown a second head.

"Thank you, sir. It's been a hell of a day." The exhaustion was honest enough. No one was that good an actor.

"I just have a few questions then we'll get you to the infirmary."

"Yes, sir," Karis said. "Though I don't know what I can tell you that I haven't told everyone else."

"That's fine, I prefer to hear the story directly from the source. Old fashioned that way I guess. Just start from the beginning."

"We were between arrivals and the three of us were standing outside the guardhouse. I was closest to the city gate, behind my sergeant and the lieutenant. As a family approached on foot someone struck me from behind and I fell flat on my face, breaking my nose, or so the medics tell me. I can't remember anything after the first blow."

Yarik gave an encouraging nod. Maybe it happened that way, but he'd seen plenty of broken noses over the years and that one looked like a fist made it. Despite the expression people seldom fell flat on their face.

"And the approaching family, what did they look like?"

"A husband and wife, I assumed, along with their daughter. The women had dark hair and light dresses. The husband sported a thick salt-and-pepper beard and tan clothes. They looked like ordinary people to me."

Yarik nodded. "I don't suppose you know what became of them? They might have information about your attackers."

"Sorry, sir. I didn't see where they went."

Yarik clapped him on the back. "That's quite alright, son. Get yourself checked out."

He left the guard and walked toward his car. Something about this felt wrong, but he couldn't put his finger on what.

"Is everything alright, Agent?" The officer had tagged along with him as he walked.

"I'm not certain. Assign someone to keep an eye on our survivor. Discreetly. I want to know where he goes and who he talks to. Maybe it's my overactive imagination, but better safe than sorry."

"I'll see to it personally," the officer said.

"Excellent." Yarik rattled off his cellphone number. "If anything interesting comes up you can reach me at that number."

Yarik left the officer writing on the back of his hand and slid behind the wheel of his car. He needed to find the witch. He had to assume their quarry had entered the city.

* * *

Anya had herself reasonably under control when someone knocked on the bathroom door. When Mom opened it they found Fedor waiting with a bag slung over his shoulder. "You two ready? We've only got half an hour to meet our ride."

"We're coming." Mom stuffed the bloody dress in Anya's almost-empty bag and handed it to her. "It'll be okay."

Anya nodded and they left the bathroom. Fedor stood a few feet away. She couldn't guess what was in the large canvas duffle bag slung over his shoulder, but the way things had been going it was probably filled with machine guns and hand grenades.

"What news?" Mom asked.

"The city's buzzing with security officers and at least three White Witches. They have our descriptions, but there are a lot of blond girls and men with beards in the city so that'll slow them down some. The truck's waiting out by the rear loading dock."

They followed Fedor past a few empty tables and through a swinging door that led to a kitchen. Now that she'd collected herself the food didn't smell so bad and she realized she hadn't eaten since the biscuit that morning.

"Can we grab a snack?" Anya asked.

"No time," Fedor said. "I have plenty of provisions. When we're away from the city we can eat."

Fedor pushed through another set of doors and they stepped out onto a loading dock. An unmarked panel truck had backed up to the dock, its rear door open. The interior held dozens of pieces of furniture.

Up against the wall was a large, dark trunk. Fedor opened the lid and motioned her over. "This one's for you."

Anya stood rooted in place. "You want me to hide in there?"

"Don't worry," Fedor said. "It has a false bottom. Even if the security agents search it they won't see you. Come on."

Mom nudged her and Anya hurried over. The inside looked awfully dark. Fedor reached in and lifted out the false bottom.

"It's only for a little while." He took her hand and Anya stepped inside. It was far deeper than it looked on the outside.

"Sit down and I'll put the panel back."

Anya folded her legs underneath her and ducked her head a little. Fedor put a thin panel of wood on top of her and everything went black.

A vibration ran through the floor. It was oddly soothing, a reminder that she wasn't alone in a black void. Anya hugged herself, chilled despite the warmth of the close interior. When that guard had looked at her with those cold eyes she'd known they were doomed. When the rebel killed him there was a moment, just a moment, of relief. She had her freedom, at least for a little while longer. It only cost the lives of two men.

Was her freedom worth it? She liked to imagine they were evil men. Certainly the older officer had the look of a villain. It helped a little. If they were just a pair of unlucky pawns working the wrong checkpoint at the wrong time and they died because she showed up, she wasn't sure how to deal with that. Anya forced the thought to the back of her mind. Better for everyone if she didn't think about it.

* * *

The Dragon Temple wasn't an actual place of worship. Religion was outlawed in the Empire. The only god here was the czar himself. The people called it the Dragon Temple because of the giant dragon statue sitting right between the steps leading up to the doors.

Yarik parked, levered himself out of the car, and marched across the sidewalk in front of the building. He looked up at the ten-story white-stone building and grimaced. The place had to be crawling with witches. Igor and the boys didn't even bother getting out of their car, lucky stiffs.

He climbed the ten steps and pushed through the doors. Inside was a reception area that would have been at home in any government building in the Empire. A desk with a middle-aged woman seated behind it rested in the middle of a white-tiled chamber. Her hair was pulled back in a tight bun and a pair of tiny round glasses perched on the end of her nose.

There wasn't another soul in sight and the silence gave him the creeps. At least he wouldn't have to wait in line. He doubted anyone came here unless compelled.

Well, best get on with it. He went over to the desk and plastered a smile on his face.

The secretary looked at him without expression. "Yes?"

"Senior Agent Yarik to see Irmina."

"She's expecting you, I assume?"

Yarik nodded.

"One moment." She picked up the phone, hit three numbers, and waited. "There's an Agent Yarik here to see you. As you wish."

She hung up the phone. "She'll be down shortly. Wait by the door, but don't get in the way."

"Sure, wouldn't want to hold up any of your many visitors."

Yarik stood beside the door and ignored the secretary's glare. She wasn't a witch and he owed her no more than common courtesy.

Ten minutes later a hole opened in the ceiling and Irmina floated down. She appeared fully composed after her encounter with the rebels.

She landed beside him. "Have you found them?"

"No, but I think they're inside the city." He told her about the incident at the checkpoint. "It can't be a coincidence."

"Agreed. I've sent wind spirits to scour the city. There's some unusual activity at the train yard. Given their obvious desire to escape the Empire, that would be an excellent place to start."

Dorcha served as a transport hub for three connected counties. Hundreds of trains came and went every day, both passenger and cargo. It would take forever to search every one. Lucky they had magic on their side.

"Do you have some trick to locate them?" he asked.

"I suspect they'll reveal themselves with the proper incentive." He shivered at the way she said incentive. "On our way we'll stop at the barracks and call out the reserves. When three hundred city guards pour into the yard they'll have to react. Once we capture a few of them, it won't be difficult to pry loose the knowledge we need."

While he hated working with witches, Yarik was glad to be on the same side as Irmina. At least for the moment.

* * *

Yarik coughed as they approached the rail yard. The diesel exhaust from hundreds of train engines put a thick haze in the air. It was a wonder the workers didn't all suffer from lung diseases. Ahead of him, three columns of fifty guardsmen each marched in lockstep, their rifles slung over their shoulders. Though their heavy tread was loud, the noise from the trains dwarfed it by several orders of magnitude. He wished he'd thought to bring ear plugs.

So far no one had done anything aggressive. In fact, everyone that had seen them ran in the opposite direction, an entirely prudent decision even for those guilty of nothing beyond having bad luck.

Irmina had brought along a pair of her sister witches and the three of them flew in the air overhead, probably busy searching with magic. Yarik hadn't the slightest idea how that worked and was just as happy to have them in the air out of his way.

The column came to a stop at the central junction where ten lines came together and a complex system of switches sent the trains to their proper destinations.

"All right." Yarik had to shout so the men could hear him over the trains. "You all know what the targets look like, fan out and find them. Remember, we want the girl alive. The rest, well, use your own judgement."

The guards spread out in squads and quickly disappeared amidst the boxcars. Igor and the boys stayed with Yarik.

"Should we help, sir?" Igor asked.

"No, we brought the guards to handle the grunt work. We'll stay here and coordinate."

"By coordinate you mean we'll wait until they catch the target then swoop in and snatch her, right?" Igor asked.

"Not at all." Yarik grinned. "I'm sure Irmina and her friends will grab the girl long before we arrive. We're going to listen for gunfire and explosions. Should we hear any we'll contact the teams and send them in the proper direction. I certainly have no intention of getting shot in this filthy excuse for a city."

"Amen to that, sir," Igor said.

Barely ten minutes had passed when the first explosion sounded. It wasn't an especially big one, probably a hand grenade. It came from Yarik's left. He squinted through the haze, but saw nothing but more haze.

He raised his radio. "Possible encounter in quadrant three. Squads thirteen and fourteen converge."

A pair of beeps acknowledged his order. Less than a minute later the clatter of gunfire came from that direction. He hadn't expected much in the way of resistance. Either the rebels were desperate, overly eager to get the girl out, or simply couldn't pass up so many targets. Yarik suspected option three. A couple hundred targets and no civilians to get in the way, it was too perfect. A train chugged by and one of the automatic switches clanged over.

"I thought we shut those down!" Yarik said. A second train rolled out. If the trains dispersed they'd never track down the girl.

"We did shut it down," Igor said. "But they're all computer controlled. A simple command could get them moving again no problem."

"Didn't we leave guards in the control room?"

Igor nodded. "Six of them."

A gust of wind pelted Yarik with gravel. A moment later a screaming man went flying into the sky. Looked like the witches had gotten into the scrum.

"Let's check out the control room." Yarik drew his pistol and led the way.

More trains set out by the second. Everywhere Yarik looked he found movement. It would be hard to separate a real threat from a shifting shadow. This was why he joined the security services instead of the army. Close-quarters combat with a desperate enemy was a good way to get yourself killed.

The control room sat at the top of a tower overlooking the yard. By some act of good fortune they reached the base of it without getting shot at. From the sounds coming from deeper in the yard the guards weren't so lucky.

A door built into the tower swung back and forth in the witches' wind. He grabbed the handle and looked closer. Someone had smashed the lock. He glanced at Igor and found his second had drawn his automatic as had the boys behind him.

Yarik cocked the hammer on his revolver, met the anxious gazes of each of his subordinates, and nodded.

He shoved the door open and lunged through. Inside was an empty room with an iron staircase leading up to the control room. A pair of bodies, their white uniforms stained red, lay at the base of the steps. That answered one of his questions.

The step squeaked when he put his weight on it. Yarik grimaced and shifted so his foot was as close to the wall as he could put it. He tried again and was rewarded with silence. One painful step at a time he worked his way up.

The first landing was empty as was the second. At the top of the third set of steps, a closed door waited. He listened hard, but heard nothing beyond the muted sounds of battle outside. Well, he couldn't hold off any longer.

Yarik pointed at Igor then at the door. His second frowned, but moved ahead of him. The boys went up next and Yarik brought up the rear. Not the bravest move, but he had a wife to think about. Besides, his younger subordinates had quicker reflexes.

Igor tiptoed up to the closed door and tried the handle. He shook his head.

Terrific, it was locked. An idea popped into his head. Before he could think too hard about it Yarik stomped up the steps and knocked.

An annoyed voice said, "What?"

"The Kazakovs are safely away," Yarik said. "We need to withdraw."

"That wasn't the plan." The door opened and Yarik shot a youngster with a thin beard right between the eyes.

They charged through.

Yarik shot a man raising his machine gun.

Beside him Igor fired as fast as his finger could work the trigger and the boys did too. When they'd emptied their weapons the control room was silent. Bodies decorated the floor and control panel. Blood spattered everything.

Yarik grimaced. What a mess. "Stop those trains, Igor."

Igor dragged one of the bodies off the controls. "No can do, sir."

"Why not?"

"Rebels locked everything on automatic then smashed the override controls. It was done before we got here."

"So this was nothing but a waste of time." Yarik holstered his gun.

"We did kill some rebels, sir."

Yarik appreciated Igor's attempt to make him feel better, but a handful of dead rebels wasn't going to help them complete their mission.

"Can you at least access the computer and get a printout of where every train is bound?"

"No problem. I can even sort them for you if you'd like."

"Put everything headed west at the top. If they're trying to escape the Empire that's the way they'll be going."

* * *

When the lid on her secret compartment went up, the light almost blinded Anya. She'd been lying there trembling in fear ever since she heard the first explosion. When her vision came back into focus she found Fedor and her mother looking down at her. Her mind finally cleared enough that she noticed the vibration in the floor and rumble of wheels on the track.

Fedor reached down and helped her out. Anya's legs wobbled after so long cooped up in the small space. She stepped out of the trunk and took a few steps. Everything still seemed to work.

"What happened? When I heard those explosions I feared the worst."

"The security forces figured out how we planned to escape," Fedor said. "Fortunately The Manager assumed they would and made the necessary preparations. We should be okay for a while. You may as well get comfortable, it's a long ride to Anapa."

The boxcar they'd stowed away on was filled with crates, but there really wasn't anywhere to sit. She paced around, trying to get the blood flowing and settle her nerves.

When she stopped she said, "They're going to find us again, aren't they?"

Fedor was a large, dark presence in the shadowy container. "Probably. Security agents are nothing if not determined. If they do find us it may come to a fight. Are you up for it?"

Anya restrained a hysterical giggle. She'd never been in a real fight in her life. Her biggest challenges up until this was physics homework and trying to decide whose invitation to the Summer Dance to accept. Now she found herself on the run from a government that planned to turn her into a slave. She wanted to cry, but refused to indulge her weakness. Maybe she wasn't up to it, but she was damn sure not going down without a fight.

Mom started to come to her, but Fedor held her back.

"I don't know," she said at last. "But I intend to try. Can you teach me to fight?"

He chuckled and she heard his smile. "I certainly can. To shoot too if you'd like."

Anya nodded to herself. "I'd like that very much."

5

ANAPA AND THE SEA

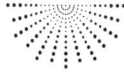

Yarik tossed the pile of printouts down on his borrowed desk. There were fifty trains headed for various destinations to the west of Dorcha and any one of them could be carrying the targets. How was he supposed to narrow it down? Hell, they could swap trains at any of a handful of stops along the line. It was like looking for a needle in a haystack.

The file on Fedor wasn't much more useful. Huge chunks of time, sometimes months, were unaccounted for. Yarik wanted to pull his hair out.

He stood up, leaned back, and popped his spine into alignment. It felt like he'd been staring at those damn papers forever. All around the Dorcha security building guards and agents shuffled papers, tapped away at keyboards, and chatted with their comrades while drinking bad coffee. It wasn't so different from home.

Yarik hissed through gritted teeth and went to get a cup of

the sludge they passed off as coffee. He needed to get this sorted if he wanted to see his wife again before winter. At least Irmina seemed content to spend her time at the temple rather than looming over him. Maybe she'd magic up a solution to their problem.

Maybe, but probably not. In his experience magic had as many limits as it did uses. Not that it didn't have a lot of uses, just not many that applied to investigations of mundane matters.

A pair of guards nodded to him as he approached the coffee maker and moved aside to give him room. After three days his mystique as a senior agent had faded and the men came to realize he was just a guy like them. It was nice that they no longer felt the need to cringe when he looked their way.

He took a sip and winced at the bitter, burnt flavor. The pollution in the train yard had left a better taste in his mouth. Maybe he could requisition some used oil from the motor pool. It couldn't help but be an improvement.

"Sir?" Igor came hurrying up. The boys had returned yesterday to keep an eye on things back home so all he had was his second to rely on.

"Please tell me you have some good news."

"I don't know if it's good, but it's news. The guard from the checkpoint you wanted watched made contact with a known resistance sympathizer. Though the guard trailing him didn't get close enough to overhear the conversation he did pinch the sympathizer and bring him in for questioning."

"I assume someone is still following the guard."

"Yes, sir. The prisoner is in an isolation cell waiting for you. I figured you'd want to handle the questioning yourself."

"You figured right. Good job, Igor. Let's go have a chat with our guest." They left the open work area and made their way to the holding cells.

Isolation Room Three held a pimply-faced kid that couldn't have been more than sixteen. Yarik restrained a groan. He doubted this kid knew his ass from a hole in the ground, much less anything useful.

"This is the resistance sympathizer?"

"Yes, sir." Igor consulted a file. "He's been arrested twice for painting antigovernment graffiti on public buildings."

"A graffiti artist. And he's our only lead." Yarik wanted to bang his head against the wall. "Well, let's see what he has to say."

Igor unbolted the door and Yarik pushed through. The kid stiffened on his cheap plastic chair. The handcuff connecting him to the bolted-down table jingled when he moved.

"So what do you know about the resistance?" Yarik asked.

"Nothing, sir, I swear. I haven't tagged a building in months. I'm keeping my nose clean, just like the sergeant told me to."

"Then what were you and Guard..." Yarik looked at Igor. "What was his name again?"

"Karis, sir."

"Right, what were you and Guard Karis talking about just before you were brought in?"

The look of confusion on the kid's face almost made Yarik laugh. "Who's Guard Karis?"

"The guy you were talking to just before you were brought in. Early twenties, broken nose, any of this ringing a bell?"

"You mean Anton? I hardly know the guy. He's dating my sister and wanted me to let her know he couldn't make dinner tonight."

"Why didn't he just call?" Yarik asked.

"Jana works at the government office, cleaning up or whatever. No cellphones allowed. It's easier for him to tell me and I'll pass it on since I'll see her tonight when she gets off work."

"There was an incident a couple days ago," Yarik said. "Did Anton mention it?"

"Yeah, that was fucked up." The kid shook his head. "He seemed pretty jittery. Is that what all this is about?"

Yarik nodded. "We're being extra careful after the killings. Since you were a person of interest to the government we had to bring you in, just to be sure. I'm pleased to see it was nothing and that you're continuing to behave yourself. Keep up the good work."

"Yes, sir."

"Igor."

Igor took out his key and unlocked the kid's cuffs before escorting him out of the room. Five minutes later they regrouped at Yarik's desk.

"Sorry, sir. I thought it was a break."

"It might have been. Get me everything you can find on Jana and her brother. A spy in the government offices would be a valuable thing for the resistance, don't you think?"

Igor nodded. "I'm on it."

* * *

Yarik closed the file Igor had brought him an hour ago on Jana Korova and her brother Milo, the would-be artist. It made for interesting reading. Apparently their father had been a member of the resistance. When he was caught and executed, the mother hung herself in shame leaving the children to the tender mercies of a state orphanage. If ever there was an institution capable of churning out a steady stream of rebels, that was it.

Jana showed all the precursors of a rebel sympathizer, but unlike her brother she never acted out. Not once. She got good grades in school, looked after her brother, said and did the right things. She passed the background check for her new job with no troubles. That just went to show how little imagination the government recruiters had. Yarik had no doubt about the rage Jana was hiding, the only question was, how did she let it off? If he had to guess he'd say by selling information from her job to the rebels.

What he needed to determine was whether the guard was a loyal man being used, or if he was in on it. The answer should come tonight after Milo passed news of his questioning on to his sister. If Yarik guessed right, it should be enough to set them off. Hopefully.

He pushed away from his borrowed desk and yawned. He had another long night in store. Jana got off work in five hours. Maybe he could sneak in a quick nap.

Alas it wasn't to be. He'd barely put his feet up on the desk of a conveniently empty office when a junior guard knocked and poked his head in. "There's a witch here to see you, sir."

He groaned and pushed to his feet. They had the absolute worst timing. He didn't know if it was a magic thing or not, but it felt like a curse to him. "Where is she?"

The guard looked over his shoulder. "She's on her way now."

"Thanks for the warning. You can make yourself scarce."

"Thank you, sir." The young man hurried off like a frightened rabbit. Not that Yarik blamed him.

A few seconds later the harpy in white appeared in the doorway. "Well, what have you found?"

"Not a lot, unfortunately. I'm waiting on a lead now, but if it doesn't pan out we'll be reduced to checking the fifty trains headed west one by one. Is that something your magic can help with?"

"We've been working on it, but it's difficult to get a fix on moving metal boxes. So much earth interferes with our air magic." She glowered at him. "If we had a specific target it would allow us to focus our energies."

He held his hands out in a helpless gesture. "We're doing what we can. With any luck I'll have something definite for you by tonight, but there are no guarantees."

Irmina swirled her hand and whispered something. Yarik held his breath and flinched against the coming blow. Instead a gentle breeze caressed his face.

"We can speak freely now."

Yarik hadn't realized they couldn't speak freely before. "Okay."

"News of this debacle has reached His Imperial Majesty the Dragon Czar. I suspect one of my sisters sent a message in an attempt to curry favor. His Majesty is not pleased that one of his future White Witches is displaying anything but gratitude for his favor. My orders are to resolve this and quickly."

Yarik shook his head. Did she imagine he was taking his time because he enjoyed hanging around in this industrial toilet? "I understand your desire and would never think to contradict His Majesty's command, however, there are certain aspects of an investigation that can't be rushed. If we push too hard the resistance in this city will go to ground and we'll never dig them out until the girl is long gone."

"The Dragon Czar, may he rule forever, is not always

understanding of the failings of us mere mortals. I say this not as a threat, but simply to make you understand our situation. If we fail, banishment to the eastern front is the best we can hope for." Every hint of color had drained from her already pale face.

She was scared. Yarik tried to wrap his mind around that. He'd seen witches angry, arrogant, obsessive, and cruel, but frightened was a new one for him. It made her seem almost human, vulnerable even.

He didn't know how to handle it. He looked closer at her, the dark, red-rimmed eyes, white hair, and sunken cheeks. Her white robe appeared slept in. Underneath all the arrogance and magic, she couldn't be more than twenty-two, young enough to be his daughter.

He sighed. "We'll get this sorted out then return to our boring lives. Don't worry."

She stiffened and he feared for a moment that he'd shown her too much kindness, but she relaxed again. "Thank you, Agent Yarik. You'll contact me when you know something?"

It was an honest question not an order. "I will."

* * *

Fedor held a chair cushion liberated from one of the shipping crates and braced himself. It was more to help with his balance in the shifting boxcar than worry over how hard Anya could punch. He'd been helping her with some basic combat training ever since they left Dorcha and the girl was an eager pupil, not terribly skilled, but eager.

Anya wiped sweat from her brow and raised her fists again. "Ready?" she asked.

Fedor nodded and forced himself not to smile. He refused

to do anything she might interpret as looking down on her. Unlike him, Anya hadn't been a rebel for half her life, running and fighting and hiding, always in fear for her survival. She'd enjoyed a reasonably normal life and all this had to be a horrible struggle for her, but she didn't quit or sulk and he admired her for that. Her father would be so proud.

Her fist slapped into the cushion with more force than last time. She'd begun to figure out how to set her feet to anchor herself before her blow. It was a good start. If he had a year to train her she'd make a formidable fighter. Unfortunately, he only had another week.

"Put more shoulder and hip into it," Fedor said after she'd thrown a dozen punches. "Your arm isn't strong enough by itself."

"Like this?" She rotated into a good one and knocked him partway off balance.

"Better, but you need to throw them all like that."

"When can I shoot?"

Fedor grimaced as she resumed pounding the cushion. He'd taught her how to aim with one of the empty pistols as well as how to properly squeeze the trigger, but they only had six clips of ammo and he hated to waste even a handful of shots given the danger they might be walking into. On the other hand, if Anya ever needed to use a gun it would be good for her to have at least felt the recoil of one.

"Switch to side kicks," Fedor said. "If you can give me ten perfect strikes I'll let you have three shots."

She grinned and Fedor was struck by just how young she was. Anya should have been thinking about a boyfriend and her career, not running for her life. But if there was one thing he'd learned it was that life wasn't fair.

Anya's tenth kick slammed home. The thought of getting to shoot must have inspired her. Every blow had landed perfectly.

"How was that?" Anya asked.

"Good." Fedor tossed the cushion down and went to the duffle bag. He emerged with a 9mm automatic and a loaded clip.

Sasha sat up from her place on a makeshift bed, her lips turned down in a worried frown. "Are you sure this is a good idea?"

"She needs to learn. If anything happens to us, Anya has to know how to defend herself."

"Yeah, Mom, and besides it'll be fun."

Sasha's frown didn't go away, but she nodded. Fedor held out the pistol and clip. "Show me how."

Anya took the weapon, slammed the clip into the grip, and worked the action before snapping the safety on. Just like an old pro.

"Good." Yarik looked around and spotted a slat on one of the crates with a knot in the center. He broke it off and leaned it against a pile of crates. Even if she missed the bullet would still hit wood instead of going ricocheting around the car. "Take your stance."

Anya stood in front of the board and raised the pistol, gripping with both hands like he'd showed her.

"Aim and squeeze."

The crack of the pistol was loud in the car, but her shot was good, an inch to the right of the knot.

"Again. Make the correction."

Anya nodded and squeezed. The pistol barked and this time she only missed by a quarter inch to the left.

"One more."

Anya bit her lip and fired again. The bullet punched the

knot out of the board. He didn't know how she'd do if faced with a living, breathing target, but if she found the will she could at least hit him. The weight of what they'd done to the girl struck him once more. Fedor swore to himself that he'd do whatever was needed to keep her from having to use a gun again.

* * *

Yarik shifted, trying to get comfortable on the worn-out seat of his car. He'd parked down the street from the Dorcha government building, a sprawling three-story complex made of concrete. No one had bothered to paint the building, instead leaving it to weather to a dark gray. If they'd intended to design a building to drain the life out of you the architect had succeeded beyond his wildest imagination.

At least they had a few more hours of sunlight to work with. Tracking the target without getting caught was hard enough without trying to do it at night. Especially since the Empire didn't see fit to provide them with night vision goggles.

An hour had passed and Jana's shift ended in fifteen minutes. The plan was to follow her home then see what she did when her brother passed along Karis's message. If he was right about Jana's sympathies the reaction should be interesting.

"Are you going to call the witch?" Igor slumped in the passenger seat, a pair of binoculars clutched in his hands.

"Not until I have something to tell her. We could be barking up the wrong tree here and I'd just as soon not make myself look any more of a fool than I already have."

Igor looked his way. "You think that's possible, given her history?"

"If there's one thing I'm sure of at this point in my life it's that anything is possible."

A young man with dark hair ambled down the sidewalk toward the building, his hands thrust into his pockets. Yarik frowned and squinted. Did he have a bandage on his nose?

"Is that Karis?"

Igor raised his binoculars. "It sure is. I didn't think he was going to meet her tonight."

Yarik flipped open his phone and dialed the station. When the front desk answered he identified himself and said, "Patch me through to the surveillance team watching Guard Karis."

A moment of static then, "Go ahead, Agent Yarik."

"Can you give me an update on the target's position?"

"He went inside about three hours ago and hasn't come out."

"That's interesting, because I'm looking at him now. He's loitering outside the government building, no doubt waiting for his girlfriend to emerge."

"That can't be. We've been watching his building nonstop since he went inside."

"Can you see every exit? Every window? He slipped past you somehow. Never mind, just get over here. If he snuck out they must have something planned. For god's sake keep your distance."

Yarik hung up and dialed Irmina. He suspected they'd need the witch before this night ended.

"There she is, sir," Igor said.

"Shit." Yarik tried to focus on the ringing phone and the attractive brunette walking toward Karis.

"Agent?" Irmina said.

"Things are proceeding. Can you join us in the field? We're parked outside the government building."

"I'm on my way."

"Stay in the air and follow my car. We don't want to spook them." He'd barely finished speaking when he realized he'd just given an order to a White Witch. Not good.

"Understood. I'll wait for your signal to move in."

He let out a breath. She hadn't taken offense. Either that or she was too worried to care. The latter possibility worried him.

"There they go," Igor said.

Karis and Jana walked along the street hand in hand, the very picture of a happy couple. Under other circumstances Yarik wouldn't have given them a second look. He fired up the car and eased it into gear.

"What's around here?" Yarik asked.

Igor lowered his binoculars and unfolded a map. "Not much, civil service buildings, a few restaurants and businesses. The nearest apartment block is a quarter mile away."

"Anything associated with the resistance?"

"Nothing mentioned in the files I've read." Igor reached for the radio. "I can check with headquarters."

Yarik slapped his wrist. "You know better. They monitor our frequency. We'll just have to watch them and find out."

He eased the car out of its spot and drove down the road past the walking couple. They didn't so much as look his way. He continued on, watching them in the rearview mirror. When he'd gone a block he turned down a side street and stopped.

"Follow them, Igor. Karis knows me, but I bet he didn't notice you."

"Yes, sir."

"Don't get too close and if they do anything suspicious call me."

Igor grinned. "Don't worry, sir, I can handle a pair of kids."

Yarik grunted as Igor closed the passenger side door and started up the street. Famous last words. He really hoped Igor didn't do anything stupid. He finally had him trained enough to be of some use. It would be damned inconvenient if he got himself killed.

Yarik's phone rang. "Yes?"

"I'm in position overhead," Irmina said. "I can see your second moving down the street. There's a couple across the way from him. Are they the targets?"

"Yes. I don't expect them to do anything overt on the street, but if you could back up Igor, I'd be grateful."

"Not a problem. Would you like me to leave the line open so I can keep you up to da—"

The line went dead.

"Irmina? Hello?"

Yarik switched his phone off and on then dialed her again. Nothing. He tried the surveillance unit and came up empty again.

The little readout on his phone read "no signal." In the middle of the city he should have perfect reception. The only reason he wouldn't was if someone had messed with the local antenna.

God damn it! They'd been spotted.

Yarik slammed the car into reverse and laid a track of smoking rubber down as he screeched out of the side street.

Tires squealed as he cranked the wheel and skidded around. A bullet sent cracks running through his windshield.

He flinched, slammed it into drive, and stomped the accelerator. A second round punched through his roof.

Yarik crouched down as if it would do any good and groped for the radio.

"This is Yarik. We need backup in the government district now."

"What's your location, Agent?" the dispatcher asked.

"I don't know, just send them towards the gunfire. Now!"

He dropped the mic and risked a glance over the dash. The street Igor had gone down was just ahead.

He whipped the car around. His second was pinned down behind a dumpster and Irmina was lying in the middle of the street.

More rounds peppered the car as he drove between the witch and the shadowy figures on the rooftops shooting at them.

He opened the door and rolled out beside the witch. She was bleeding from a shoulder wound and from her stomach.

God, what a mess. He tore his jacket off and jammed it hard against the stomach wound. Irmina moaned, which reassured him that she was still alive.

"Hold that tight."

She groaned, but did as he said. Yarik drew his pistol and popped up for a look.

Bullets clattered against the car forcing him back down. He counted four people for sure. Considering they had rifles and the high ground that was more than enough.

"Igor, you hurt?"

"I'm fine, sir. They shot the witch first which gave me enough warning to get down."

"I don't suppose you have a shot."

"Afraid not."

Yarik flinched when two more shots pinged off the hood. The rebels seemed content to hold them down.

Where the hell was his backup?

"Did you see where the targets went?"

"Sorry, sir," Igor said. "I got distracted."

Talk about a bad situation. He needed to get Irmina to a healer.

Thunder cracked in the clear night just before a blinding light forced him to shut his eyes. When he opened them again Yarik risked a look over the car. Two figures in white flew around the roof where the gunmen had been moments before.

Backup at last. Not the kind he'd been expecting, but for once he wasn't about to complain about witches showing up unannounced. Yarik scrambled to his feet and waved to draw their attention, yet another thing he never imagined himself doing.

The witches held their positions for another few seconds before flying in a tight arc down to the car. Both women looked older than Irmina though younger than him.

"What happened?" the older witch asked.

"Ambush. She got hit twice. I've done what I can for the bleeding, but I'm no healer."

The older witch turned a cold eye on her younger companion. "Take care of her."

The younger witch motioned Yarik out of the way and held her hands over Irmina. A golden bubble of energy surrounded her and the two of them flew off. Yarik watched them until they were out of sight.

"Will she be alright?"

"Of course, no White Witch would be slain from such minor wounds."

The wounds had looked pretty serious to Yarik, but he held his peace. "Thank you for the rescue. I expected more conventional backup."

"We overheard the call and knew one of our sisters was with you so we chose to respond. Tell me everything."

Yarik did as she bid and when he finished she said, "How did they know Irmina was there and what sort of weapon did they use to penetrate her defenses?"

"I'd very much like the answers to those questions as well. Could I persuade you to lend us your help in tracking down our missing rebels?"

A cruel smile twisted her thin lips. "I will question the dead then we will hunt down the czar's enemies and make them beg for death."

Yarik swallowed. That was more the sort of attitude he expected from a White Witch. He seldom pitied anyone stupid enough to oppose the Empire, but in that moment he felt bad for Karis and Jana. He wouldn't wish an encounter with this witch on anyone, even a pair of rebels.

* * *

Yarik, Igor, and the witch, Nosorova, marched down the street toward a closed-up food distribution center. The modest-sized, single-story building had been shut down and its inventory moved to a larger warehouse years ago. Like everything else not directly involved with members of the ruling class it was made of cement blocks with narrow windows. For some reason the Empire liked to build even the most mundane structure like it had to withstand a bomb blast.

Yarik had never understood it, but then his job didn't require him to understand his masters' foolishness, only to obey them. The witch had muttered and waved her hands then marched them down the empty street. The gun battle seemed to have scared off all the locals, a good thing for them as they didn't have to worry about any innocents getting caught in the crossfire. He wouldn't have to worry, anyway, somehow he doubted Nosorova would be overly concerned about anyone that had the misfortune to get in her way.

"Are you sure this is the place?" Yarik asked.

She shot him a glare. "Of course. I can sense magic emanating from the building and it isn't ours."

Yarik tensed up. Regular people like him were sitting ducks if the enemy had magic. If it came to a fight he doubted he and Igor would be of much help.

"How do you want to handle this? Magic is way outside my area of expertise."

"I will deal with the rebels," she said. "You two stay out here and make sure no one escapes."

"If there are multiple exits we might miss someone," Yarik said. "Maybe we should wait for the second surveillance team to arrive."

"There's no time." She whistled and gestured. Yarik didn't see anything, but he assumed she'd accomplished something. "There, I've placed guardians on the other side of the building. You two need only worry about this one. I trust you can handle that much at least."

"You bet. Good luck."

She sniffed. "When you have magic, luck is unnecessary."

Nosorova strutted across the street like she hadn't a fear in the world. Surprising considering Irmina had just been shot by these rebels. Did she think acting fearless would intimidate any watching rebels or was she stupid enough to believe Irmina had simply been careless? All he knew for sure was that having two witches get shot while working with him wouldn't be good for his career or his life.

"I liked the other one better," Igor said.

Yarik nodded, but didn't speak. If the witch was using magic to listen in on them he didn't want to say anything that might set her off.

Across the street Nosorova reached the door and waved her hand. Nothing happened.

She made a more complex motion and pointed at the door. A light flashed, but still nothing happened to the door.

"Nosorova seems to be experiencing technical difficulties." Igor grinned, seeming thoroughly amused by her troubles.

Yarik wasn't amused in the least. Anything that gave a White Witch problems would probably kill a pair of security agents with no difficulty.

Finally she stomped her foot, looked their way, and waved for them to join her.

"So much for watching the door." Yarik led the way across the street at a flat-out run, his head on a swivel. They reached the door without encountering any resistance. That was a stroke of good luck.

"Is there a problem?" he asked.

"Obviously there's a problem." She jabbed a bony finger at the door as though accusing it of a crime. "The rebels have acquired a dark magic ward and it's blocking my magic. You two will have to enter and arrest everyone inside while I keep watch."

"We need to wait for reinforcements," Yarik said. "There's no way to know how many rebels are inside and if we don't have your magic to back us up we'll be sitting ducks."

"I told you there isn't time. The longer we wait the better the chances of them escaping."

"No one can escape with your magic surrounding the building. We can have an entry team here in ten minutes. Please."

Her expression hardened. "Get in there and do your job or so help me I'll have you before the Court of Corruption on insubordination charges."

Goddamn witches.

Yarik drew his revolver. "Alright, Igor, put your boot to that door and let's get at it."

Igor pulled his automatic, reared back, and kicked the door right below the handle. The frame crunched and burst inward.

Yarik lunged through into an empty hall. Nothing there but an old mat and some coat hooks hanging from the wall. He listened hard, but heard only silence.

He eased down the hall with Igor right behind him. Dim light from the door barely revealed an empty room beyond the hall. This must have served as an office for the warehouse. At the rear was another door that led to the main storage room.

Yarik glanced at Igor and nodded toward the door. Igor eased over and reached for the handle. It turned without a sound. Slowly, slowly he eased the door open. Voices came from inside, but Yarik couldn't make out what they were saying.

Once Igor had the door open he slipped through and Yarik tiptoed in, shutting the door behind him. The storage room wasn't anywhere near as empty as he'd expected. The two agents crouched behind crates and sacks that had been piled up haphazardly to one side of the door.

In the center of the room a small table held a large stone covered with squiggly marks that pulsed with energy he felt more than saw. That had to be whatever was giving Nosorova fits.

Five people stood in a circle around the stone, including Jana and Karis. Of even greater interest to Yarik was the handful of machine guns leaning on the table between the rebels. He didn't care much for their odds, even with surprise.

"I can't return to work now," Jana said. "The security forces are clearly on to me, Karis too."

"Calm down," said an older man with a gray beard in grease-covered overalls. "We'll find new places for both of you, new identities, you'll be fine."

Igor raised his gun, but Yarik gave a shake of his head. He wanted to see how this played out.

"Has anyone heard from Fedor?" one of the strangers asked.

Yarik perked up at that. Maybe he'd finally get that lead he'd been after.

"No," Graybeard said. "They won't make contact until they've reached the boat in Anapa, too much danger of the government intercepting."

That was all he needed to hear. It made sense, the port of Anapa was one of the busiest in the western half of the Empire. If you were trying to sneak out, you couldn't hope for a better place. Maybe the witches would have a way of tracking the girl, otherwise he didn't know how they'd find her.

Yarik cocked the hammer of his pistol as quietly as he could, steeled himself, popped up, and shot the black stone. It exploded in a shower of gravel.

Igor put two rounds in one of the strangers before the rest dove for their rifles.

Yarik ducked behind the crates just before a fusillade of bullets tore into them. He hoped whatever was in the crates was heavy duty, hopefully steel.

There was a loud blast and streams of light poured into the room. The machine guns clattered on full auto, but they weren't hitting the crates.

Yarik risked a glance and found the witch descending

through a hole in the roof. Bullets ricocheted off an invisible barrier as she descended like an angel of death.

She waved a hand and a gust of wind picked up Jana and Karis and hurled them across the room like so much litter.

The man with the beard flung his rifle aside and leapt for one of the crates opposite Yarik.

Lightning cracked and a rebel exploded in a shower of sizzling gore.

The last man broke and ran. He might as well not have bothered. Nosorova made a twirling gesture and what looked like a mini tornado sprang to life around him. He clawed at his throat and after a moment went still.

Yarik was so distracted by all the magic that he almost forgot about the bearded man. Movement drew his eye back in time to see him emerge from the crate with a long-barreled, single-shot pistol. He leveled it at the witch.

Yarik fired an instant before him, blowing his brains all over the sacks behind him.

Nosorova landed and looked around at the mess. "Fine shot, Agent, though I assure you I was in no danger from a simple gun."

"I had a bad feeling." Yarik holstered his pistol. "He was awfully anxious to get his hands on that weapon—so anxious that he abandoned a machine gun to dig it out."

He crossed the room and took the gun from the dead man's hand. Yarik clicked the trigger to half cock, lowered the breech, and extracted a large-caliber cartridge. It felt cold in his hand. He looked closer at the bullet.

"Strange, there's a skull carved into it."

"Give me that." Nosorova snatched the cartridge out of his hand. "A Death's Head bullet. This must be what they used on

Irmina. I shall have to apologize to the girl. I thought she was simply careless with her defenses."

"What's a Death's Head bullet?" Igor asked.

"It's a bullet infused with dark magic designed to pierce magical defenses," Yarik said. He'd read about them years ago, but never thought to see one. "They're better known as witch killers."

"Correct, Agent. We've seen an increase in their use over the last year. We've tracked their point of origin to Anapa, but we haven't yet figured out who exactly is smuggling the cursed things in."

"Interesting." Yarik scratched his cheek. "The target is heading to Anapa as we speak. Coincidence, you think?"

"I do not believe in coincidences, Agent."

"Neither do I. I believe we have our next destination. Igor, how do you feel about flying?"

* * *

The train lurched and came to a full stop. Anya couldn't wait to get out and move under her own power again. She'd never been this far from home, in fact she'd never been more than fifty miles from home before. The whole trip might have been fun if government agents weren't hunting them. Nothing like having an entire Empire trying to turn you into a slave to suck the joy out of life.

"Back in the trunk," Fedor said. "Our contact will be here soon."

Anya grimaced. She really didn't want to get crammed into that box. It felt like a coffin. "Do I have to?"

"Yes, now."

Mom came over to help her. "Just one more time, kiska.

Tonight we'll be out on the Black Sea and the Empire nothing but a memory. Can you imagine it? Water as far as you can see, the smell, the sun, fish leaping into the air. Keep that image in mind and the trunk won't be so bad."

"Hurry, Sasha, someone's coming."

Mom lifted off the lid to the secret compartment and helped her into the cramped darkness. Anya tried to imagine the sea as she lay curled up in the dark, but failed. All she could think about was being found and shot.

She wished Fedor had let her keep one of the pistols, but he wasn't confident in her ability to use it yet. It wasn't her aim that was the problem, she'd gotten to be a pretty good shot, it was her willingness to shoot someone he questioned. Not that Anya blamed him. She wasn't sure if she could do it either. Still, the cool metal in her hand would be welcome.

Time passed in the dark. Twice she was jostled and jolted. There was the rumble and vibration of a truck, then voices a couple times. Whenever she heard anyone she held her breath for fear that an inspector might hear her breathing.

The trunk shifted and settled with a final thump. More voices then the lid was lifted and Fedor's bearded face appeared in the blinding light.

He held out his hand. "We're safe, for the moment."

Anya climbed eagerly out of the trunk. Even if it meant her life she swore she'd never get in the thing again. It looked like they'd ended up in a warehouse if the huge stacks of boxes were any indication. That made a certain amount of sense. Nothing odd about delivering furniture to a warehouse after all.

In addition to Mom and Fedor, another pair of men had joined them, twins by the looks, maybe ten years older than her. They'd both attempted beards, but the patchy tufts didn't impress her. They both wore simple brown overalls that wouldn't draw a second look on the street.

Her mother hurried over and wrapped Anya in a tight embrace. When she finally let go Anya asked, "So where's the boat?"

"There's a problem," Fedor said. "Security agents are swarming the docks. Apparently they raided one of our safe houses in Dorcha and figured out our destination. They may not know exactly which ship we plan to take, but they clearly mean to stay between us and escape."

"What are we going to do?"

"That's what we're trying to figure out."

"We have two options," one of the twins said. "We can create a diversion on the side of the docks opposite the boat and try to sneak you aboard in the chaos, or we can leave Anapa, drive up the coast, and meet the boat out at sea. Both options have serious downsides, but I can't think of anything else."

Anya looked at each of them in turn, but found only crinkled brows and downcast eyes. If they weren't confident, how was she supposed to feel?

A door crashed open and a young woman burst into the warehouse. "There's a witch coming this way."

"Is it a sweep or is she coming directly at us?" Fedor asked.

"Right at us, like an arrow. She's holding something. I didn't get a good look at it, but whatever it is, it's leading her and two squads of city guards this way. You need to go."

"Well, that settles it," Fedor said. "We break for the docks. Contact the other cells and let them know we're moving now. I want fire teams waiting for us at the primary rally point in fifteen minutes."

"Captain Gustav's expecting us and ready to go at a moment's notice," the second twin said.

"Good. We're not going to have much of a lead on the Empire's dogs." Fedor strode toward the rear of the warehouse. "Let's move."

Anya never would have believed she'd feel grateful for the arrival of a witch, but the shock of it seemed to jar everyone out of their concerns and pushed them to act. Maybe it would work out well and maybe not, but at least they were moving and that made her feel better. The trick was not to think about what they were moving towards.

* * *

Gulls cried on the bright blue day. Behind Yarik two hundred plus boats bobbed at their slips. They ranged from two-man skiffs to seventy-yard-long fishing trawlers. Three hundred city guardsmen in crisp white uniforms had searched every one of them yesterday and today and found nothing. Wherever the rebels were, it wasn't here.

Maybe the show of force would scare them off. Part of him hoped it did and another part, the larger part, hoped they did something stupid and got caught so he could go home. He missed his wife and their little cabin. He missed getting home at night for a warm meal and sleeping in his own bed. If the Empire allowed it he'd retire tomorrow.

Yarik took a sidelong glance at Irmina. The young witch seemed well enough, if a little pale, paler anyway. Her recovery was a testament to the skill of the Dragon Temple's healers. They'd restored full movement to her shoulder and he'd already seen her cast several spells. None of that simple stuff concerned him.

What did concern him was how she'd react in a fight. After getting wounded there was every possibility she'd panic at the first sign of combat. He'd seen it before in young soldiers. Some powered through and others never recovered enough to fight. Hopefully she'd be okay, or at least okay enough that she didn't get him killed.

They'd taken up position along with Igor and a third of Anapa's city guard at the docks. If their information was correct, and he felt pretty sure it was, the resistance intended to smuggle the girl out by boat. He couldn't think of a better way to do it. The only other path out of the Empire was over a rugged mountain range that swarmed with frost wolves.

He shivered at the thought of having to fight the white-furred brutes. He'd seen a stuffed one at a museum years ago. It stood five feet tall at the shoulder, weighed over six hundred pounds, and breathed a mist that if it hit you would freeze the blood in your veins. No, leaving by boat was definitely the way to go.

When he peeked at Irmina a second time she caught him. "I'm fine, Agent. I don't need you fussing over me like a mother hen."

"Someone needs to." Since she'd revealed her vulnerable side Yarik found he had a hard time lumping her in with all the other witches. "Nosorova barely looked at you when you arrived. I figured since you all talk about being sisters she might have been more worried."

Irmina looked around and Yarik mimicked her. The nearest person was Igor and he was twenty paces away whistling an off-color shanty.

"I don't know how much you know about the White Witches, but while we're sisters, united against all enemies of the Empire, we're also competitors, always striving to outdo one another and gain status in the eyes of the czar. Power and authority all flow through him. His current favorite leads the order and those out of favor end up in the middle of nowhere."

"Is that how you ended up answering my call?"

She offered a weak smile and for a second he saw the young woman instead of the witch. "I've come to like you, Agent Yarik, so I'll tell you the truth. I'm not, by a far measure, the strongest member of the organization and getting shot isn't going to do my status any favors. Unless I do something remarkable, like capture a runaway candidate, I'll spend the rest of my life a thousand miles from the capital doing nothing worthwhile."

"There's something to be said for the quiet country life. It's much calmer, less politics, fewer rebels. Before this little outburst I hadn't been shot at for fifteen years. Assuming I live, I'd be happy to go another fifteen."

"My ambition runs a little higher than that. At a minimum I'd like to serve in the capital someday."

Ambition was a fine way to get yourself killed, but judging by the set of her jaw explaining that wouldn't get him anywhere. "Well, I wish you the best of luck."

"You're a very poor liar, Agent, but thank you just the same."

An explosion ripped through the quiet morning. Flames blossomed three hundred yards from their post. Irmina turned and ran, but before she'd gone three steps Yarik said, "Wait!"

She spun to face him. "Wait? The resistance is attacking the docks. They're obviously trying to force their way through to the escape ship."

"Whatever the Empire may think of the rebels, they're not stupid. That has to be a distraction. If you take to the air and hide yourself we'll get out of sight down here. I suspect we'll get a nice surprise."

She chewed her lip and looked again toward the drifting smoke and crack of rifles. "Should one of my sisters capture the runaway my hopes for advancement die."

Yarik shrugged. "Igor, are there any good hiding places around here?"

"Yes, sir. There are shipping containers stacked against the warehouse at the edge of the docks. We can hide there and see anyone approaching."

"Good man." Yarik clapped Igor on the shoulder. "Let's go."

"I will keep watch from above." Irmina flew up, slowly fading from sight as she did so.

Yarik grinned as he ran for the warehouse. Learning to trust others was a difficult thing for witches. In fact, most never learned how to do it. Maybe there was hope for this one yet.

* * *

Fedor parked their borrowed car a block from the docks in a parking lot facing an empty public beach. According to the local resistance the guards had ordered the beach cleared and closed when they started to search the area. The locals hadn't been thrilled, but they weren't stupid enough to say anything.

Anya sat in the back seat and peered at the many boats bobbing in the water. Which of them would carry them out of this awful place? She didn't know, though she hoped it was one of the bigger ones. Maybe the luxury yacht with the blacked-out windows. She could see herself lying on the deck and enjoying the sun along with her freedom.

Her gaze shifted to take in the many figures in white that dotted the area. There had to be at least a hundred guards protecting the ships. Hopefully the rebel cells preparing to attack would be enough to get their attention.

Fedor checked his watch then took out a set of binoculars. "Any minute now."

Anya chewed her thumbnail. It seemed like they spent a lot of time waiting. Much as she hated the fear that came with action, she preferred it to the anticipation. Best to get it over with as soon as possible.

As if her thought caused it, a huge fireball blossomed at the far end of the pier. The distant crack of gunfire filled the air. She'd heard far too much of that over that past weeks.

"Do we go?" Mom asked. She had her hand on the door handle.

"Not yet." Fedor didn't lower his goggles. "Let them get fully engaged."

They waited two minutes, then five. Anya's stomach twisted and her heart raced. *Let's just do it already!* She wanted to scream it at the top of her lungs, but she swallowed the words and waited. Fedor had seen them safely through up to now and she'd trust him to continue to do so.

"Now."

Everyone piled out of the car. Anya and her mother had abandoned their bags at the warehouse. Anything that might slow their escape was left behind. Anya had balked at first, but then decided she didn't want anything that might remind her of the Empire. She could start fresh wherever they ended up.

"I should have asked this before," Fedor said. "But you two can swim, right?"

Anya blanched. Her class had spent two weeks learning the basics in the Black Rock River three years ago and she hadn't been in the water since. She knew how to keep her head above water, but that was about it.

"We'll manage," Mom said.

Fedor nodded and led the way down to the shore. He kept right on going, wading into the water up to his chest before setting out at an angle from the beach with powerful strokes. The cool water raised goosebumps on her legs.

When the water reached her waist Anya hesitated.

Mom put a hand on her shoulder. "You can do it, kiska. Just stay beside me."

Anya nodded and they lunged out into the water together. She paddled frantically with her hands and feet, using the crude dog paddle her teacher had demonstrated.

Slowly, but steadily she followed along in Fedor's wake. She had just enough presence of mind to wonder how the big man had learned to swim so well. Perhaps she'd ask him on the boat. Beside her Mom glided along with a smooth sidestroke, her gaze never straying from Anya. She felt a little better knowing her mother was keeping an eye on her.

Ahead of them Fedor had stopped and was treading water. They paused beside him.

"This is where it gets tricky," he said. "Our boat is the fifty-foot trawler with a black hull. We need to approach with a minimum of splashing. If any of the Imperials have half a brain they'll have left someone to keep an eye on the boats. Watch me and if I dive, you dive. Okay?"

Anya and her mother nodded. Swimming underwater couldn't be any harder than swimming at the surface, right? At this point she was willing to do anything to leave the water behind. If she had to swim underwater, so be it.

Fedor set out again, this time using a weird stroke that made hardly a splash and left his eyes barely out of the water. She tried to emulate him, but had a hard time coordinating her arms and legs. She made progress, slow progress, but at least she was quiet.

A shadow flashed across the water ahead of them and Fedor dove beneath the surface. Anya held her breath, said a little prayer, and followed. She clawed her way down, trying to ignore the odd distortions waving in her vision.

They floated ten feet below the surface. Anya clamped her jaw shut so tight it ached. Her lungs burned and just when she thought they'd burst Fedor pointed to the surface. Anya kicked for all she was worth and burst from the water gasping for air. She fought not to cough for fear of the noise and managed a strangled croak.

When she'd collected herself they swam on. How far was this stupid boat anyway? It felt like they'd been in the water forever.

Ten minutes later Fedor stopped. Just ahead of them was a black-hulled boat. He held a finger to his lips and dove again. When her mother didn't make a move to follow she didn't either. Three dull thumps sounded in the water. Fedor swam to the surface a moment later.

He looked up at the boat. What was the holdup? Anya's teeth chattered and her eyes stung. Finally someone appeared on deck and tossed a rope ladder over the side.

Fedor waved her over. Anya swam up and grabbed the lowest rung. Somewhere out of sight another explosion sounded. She'd been so intent on not drowning she'd lost all track of the battle. Fedor gave her a boost and she managed to get her foot on a rung. She scrambled up the ladder and soon a rough hand grasped hers and pulled her over the rail.

Anya collapsed on the deck and stared at the sky. They'd

done it. She could hardly believe, in fact she might not really believe it for days, but still they'd made it.

Mom sat beside her and took Anya's hand. They shared a weary smile. Finally Fedor joined them up on deck. Anya chuckled. He looked like an otter with his hair and beard soaked and plastered to his head.

"What say we get out of here?" the man that had helped them out of the water said.

That sounded like an excellent idea to Anya. She shivered as the wind swirled and a cloud passed over the sun. She looked up in time to see the witch flying right toward them.

* * *

Yarik peeked around the side of the container at the empty docks. He'd been sure the rebels would try to sneak in on the far side of the battle. It was exactly the sort of thing they liked to do; misdirection and stealth were the best methods to use when facing a superior foe. So where the hell were they? The battle still raged at the opposite end of the pier, machine guns clattered and an explosion went off now and then.

Maybe he'd been wrong. Maybe they were planning to fight their way through the guards and escape that way. He shook his head. No, that just didn't make sense. The rebels wouldn't try and force their way through three witches and almost three hundred guards. Someone had to be coming this way.

"Sir, the witch."

Yarik spotted Irmina immediately as she plunged down toward a black-hulled trawler. What was she doing? Had she spotted something he missed? The only way that made sense was if the rebels had come from the sea.

He slapped his palm against his head. He'd never even considered that they might try to swim to the boat.

Yarik drew his pistol and burst out from around the pallets.

He sprinted toward the boat, heart pumping and feet pounding.

A shot fired.

The boat started up and pulled away from the dock.

What was she doing? The target was escaping.

Yarik fired three shots into the side of the hull, but they pinged off. The pilot wasn't visible from his position.

Once the boat cleared the pilings it accelerated out to sea. By the time he reached the end of the dock the boat was long gone.

He stomped the planks. Damn it! They'd been so close.

He looked down into the water. Irmina floated fifteen feet from the dock surrounded by a spreading pool of blood.

Yarik tossed his gun to the ground and leapt in. He swam out, grabbed her, and pulled her back to the waiting Igor. Between the two of them they heaved her up onto the dock.

He levered himself up and out of the water. "How is she?"

Igor shook his head. "Dead, sir. The bullet went right through her heart. Whoever fired it was a better shot than the sniper in Dorcha."

He slammed his fist on the dock. The one witch he actually liked and she had to go and get herself killed. This incident wasn't going to go well for him either. While he hadn't been directly responsible, she had been working with him and if there was any way for the witches to pin her death on him, Yarik was sure they'd take it. It looked bad when one of their own was killed, called their invincibility into question.

"Sir, listen," Igor said.

Yarik cocked his head. Everything was quiet. The fighting

had ended. The rebels had completed their mission and he'd failed in his.

He reached out and closed Irmina's eyes. Poor kid never had a chance. Yarik hoped he didn't end up just like her.

The more he traveled the more he realized that was life in the Empire, it used you until you had nothing left to give, like a giant leech sucking out the people's blood. You could fight it and die like the rebels or serve and hope you didn't end up bleeding on a dock somewhere. Not the best choices, but that was the Empire.

6

THE LAND OF THE NIGHT PRINCES

nya had never seen so much water. The Black Sea
stretched out in every direction. As they moved
further and further away from the Empire it felt like
a weight lifted off her shoulders. She was free, for the first time
in her life, truly free. She leaned on the rail in the front of the
boat and breathed deep of the sea air. Somehow she'd imagined it smelling fishy, but all she got was dampness and a hint
of diesel from the engine.

She'd changed out of her soaked dress and into a set of ill-
fitting men's trousers and a blue and white striped t-shirt. It
wouldn't have been her first choice of outfit, but it was dry and
she didn't complain.

Speaking of complaints, a loud gagging drew her attention
to the side rail. Mom wasn't enjoying the trip as much as she
was. Anya had taken to the ship from the moment they set out;
her mother, unfortunately, hadn't responded so well. She
seemed to prefer Anya ignore her visits to the rail, so that's
what she did.

Fedor and the man that helped them aboard—Yanni, she heard him called—emerged from the wheelhouse and climbed down to the deck. Anya went to join them.

"Everything okay?" she asked.

"So far," Fedor said. "We lost seventeen fighters at the dock plus another ten arrested."

"I'm sorry," Anya said. She had a hard time imagining all these people being willing to give up their lives to help her escape. It defied belief. Fedor said it wasn't about her, but about doing something to hurt, or at least embarrass, the Empire. That didn't do much to alleviate the guilt, but it would have to do.

"We gave as good as we got," Yanni said, a fierce smiled creasing his scarred face. "They took down three witches and over twenty guards. That's a good day's work by any standard."

Even if they were the enemy, she couldn't think of that many dead as any sort of good thing. Anya doubted she'd make much of a fighter, she was too squeamish.

Her mother pushed away from the rail and wiped her mouth with the back of her hand. "Have you seen any sign of the coast guard?"

"Are you feeling any better, Sasha?" Fedor asked.

Mom waved a dismissive hand. "I'm fine, just need a little time to get my sea legs. The coast guard?"

"No sign yet," Yanni said. "But it's only a matter of time. I've got Jacob keeping watch on the radar and listening to the radio. If they approach we'll know about it."

Mom raised an eyebrow. "And?"

"And we're no match for a cutter. Our best hope lies in speed. I've set a course straight for Constanta at maximum speed. We may look like a trawler, but this ship is rigged for speed. We'll be there in a few days at most, barring trouble."

"Then we disembark and get eaten by vampires," Anya said.

"On the contrary," Fedor said. "The princes hate the Empire almost as much as we do. They're the ones that gave us all the magical weapons we've been using to hold our own against the witches. I've made all the necessary arrangements to travel safely through their country. In fact, I found Lord Talon perfectly polite and agreeable."

"Still, it's a little like a deer trusting a pack of wolves to serve as its bodyguards. Everything's great until the guards get hungry."

* * *

"I think they're gaining." Anya stood at the rear of the ship and peered through a set of binoculars Fedor had given her. The Imperial patrol boat was little more than a dot to her naked eyes, but through the glasses its guns looked all too large.

Her mother had joined her at the rail, the worst of her seasickness having passed two days ago. "We're still well ahead. Yanni says we'll reach Constanta with time to spare."

"How much?"

"I didn't dare ask."

They'd been traveling free and clear for just under a week and Anya had hoped they'd reach their destination without any trouble when Jacob announced a blip on his radar screen, thirty miles off, but making straight for them. Yanni jammed the throttle all the way forward until the little needle went over the red line.

He noticed her worried expression, grinned, and said it didn't matter if the engine blew up as long as it lasted until they reached the port.

"Land ho!" Fedor shouted from the front of the boat.

Anya's heart leapt. Maybe they'd make it after all.

Thirty yards behind them an explosion sent a spray of water into the air. She looked back at the patrol boat. Smoke rose from the barrels of one of their guns. They didn't have to gain much to put them in range.

Yanni burst out of the wheelhouse. "Was that a shot?"

"Yeah, about thirty yards short," Anya said.

He grinned at her. "Good eye, kid. We'll make a sailor out of you yet."

"What are we going to do?" Mom asked. For the first time since this mad journey began real fear filled her voice.

"We're going to keep running. No need to worry until their shots get within five yards."

He ducked inside. Anya and her mother shared a look. Neither of them said what they were thinking, but Anya suspected it was the same thing. There was a lunatic driving the boat.

Fifteen minutes later the shots were hitting close enough to rattle the hull. Anya and her mother had abandoned their position in the rear to join Fedor up front. The docks of Constanta loomed out of a thick fog. There wasn't a single boat tied up to the piers. Further inland the warehouses had rusted years ago, their doors hanging cockeyed or in some cases having fallen to the ground. Everything cast long shadows from the setting sun.

They were sailing into a ghost town.

Anya's heart beat a little faster now that she'd seen their destination. She'd expected there'd be someone to meet them at least.

The loudest explosion yet rocked the ship. It shuddered and groaned.

Yanni and Jacob left the wheelhouse and climbed down to join them.

"We're hit," Yanni said.

"How bad?" Fedor asked.

Anya kept her eyes on the dock. They had a mile or two more to go, but the boat was already slowing.

"Bad enough." Yanni scrubbed a hand across his face. "Momentum will carry us in no problem, assuming that gunship doesn't sink us first."

Mom shot him a glare.

Yanni raised his hands in mock surrender. "I'm just saying."

A mile out another explosion shook them and the boat slowed even more.

"We're taking on water," Yanni said. "Get ready to jump on the dock as soon as we reach it and run like hell for the warehouses."

"It's not like we can hide," Anya said, her voice high and ragged in her ears.

"No need to hide." Jacob offered a reassuring smile. "The locals spend their days inside and sunset is only minutes away. Any marine stupid enough to follow us into one of those buildings will wish he'd joined the army."

Understanding dawned on her, though it did nothing to make her feel better. There were vampires living in those buildings. The plan was to run toward the blood-sucking monsters. In what world was that a good idea?

Another explosion sounded a few feet to the left of them. Apparently in this one. Better to take their chances with monsters that might want to hurt them than with men that certainly did.

The nearest pier was only a hundred feet away.

Mom held her hand in a death grip. Anya's fingers had gone

numb, but she didn't even think about asking her to loosen her hold.

"Get ready." Yanni gathered himself.

The moment the boat was even with the wooden surface he leapt. Fedor went next then Anya and her mother.

Anya's ankle wobbled and she stumbled as she struggled to keep her footing. Strong hands steadied her.

She looked up at Fedor. He nodded. "Go!"

Mom pulled on her hand and they were off and running. Anya risked a look over her shoulder. People poured off the Imperial ship, all of them armed with machine guns.

The warehouses looked impossibly far away, though it was probably only three hundred yards.

Anya had never considered herself much of an athlete, but it was amazing what fear and adrenaline could do for you.

She ran.

Her heart thumped and her lungs burned.

Bullets pinged off the ground all around them.

She crossed into the shadows stretching from the warehouses and the temperature dropped ten degrees.

"Ah!" Mom staggered and fell, jerking Anya to a stop.

She turned to see blood oozing from her mother's stomach. "Mom!"

Anya knelt and tried to press on the wound. Hot blood gushed from between her fingers.

"Run, kiska." Her mother's voice emerged in a ragged gasp. "Hurry."

"No! I'm not leaving you." She pressed harder, trying to stop the blood.

Fedor, Yanni, and Jacob had stopped as well, drawing weapons and returning fire. Anya ignored everything but her mother. She had to stop the bleeding.

It was getting so dark she couldn't see what she was doing. Something shadowy rushed past her, but she ignored that too.

Anya barely registered the change from controlled bursts of gunfire to wild, fully automatic chaos.

Fedor knelt beside her. "Let me see."

Anya moved her hands away. The night was silent. She looked up at last to find figures in black had surrounded them. They wavered, seeming solid one moment and insubstantial the next. The vampires stared at her with glowing red eyes.

"It's bad, Anya," Fedor said. "I think she's been hit in the liver. There's nothing I can do."

"My most sincere apologies." A tall man, dressed all in black like the others, separated himself from the group. "We came to help as soon as we could. I wish it had been sooner."

Fedor offered a seated bow. "Lord Talon, thank you. We'd all be dead if not for your timely aid."

Her mother moaned and twisted on the ground, her eyes clenched shut.

"Can you heal her?" Anya asked.

Lord Talon knelt beside her. "I am sorry. While we have many gifts, healing isn't among them. Light magic is painful to us. As I watched from the shadows I saw your mother shift to block the bullets from hitting you. It took great courage."

Anya had been so focused on running she hadn't even noticed when she pulled ahead of her mother. "So it's my fault." She sniffed back tears.

"No," Fedor said. "It's the Empire's fault. Don't blame yourself, Sasha wouldn't want that."

"While I can't heal her," Lord Talon said. "There is another option. A woman of such courage and beauty would be a welcome addition to the Court of Midnight."

She stared for a moment. He was offering to turn her mother into a monster. But the alternative...

"I don't know. Mom?"

Her mother opened her eyes. "I love you, kiska. Be strong on the rest of your journey."

Mom's eyes fluttered shut.

"She has almost moved beyond even my reach," Lord Talon said. "You must decide now."

"If you do this can she come with us?"

"No. Whatever happens, your mother's journey ends here. I give you my solemn promise that you will be welcome to visit my land and your mother whenever you wish."

To see her mother again was something she couldn't refuse. Maybe it was wrong, but she didn't care. "Do it."

Lord Talon's bright, white teeth flashed in the dark. He drew a long nail across his wrist and thick, dark blood welled up. He held his wrist to her mother's mouth and she drank.

Mom's body shuddered and writhed then went still. Her chest ceased to move.

"It's done," Lord Talon said. "In seven days your mother will rise and take her place among the Midnight Court."

* * *

Of all the places Yarik didn't want to visit, the Imperial capital was at the top of the list. New St. Petersburg was built from the ruins of the original city, which the elves destroyed fifteen hundred years ago during their invasion. According to the histories over twenty million people in the old country of Russia died during the war. Of course when reading an Imperial textbook it was best to take their facts with a grain of salt.

Yarik sat outside the czar's audience chamber in a modest room bigger than his whole cabin. White leather chairs and ornate end tables decorated the space. Two chairs to his left Nosorova sat and drummed her fingers on the arm of her chair. She was the only witch that had survived the disaster that was Anapa. He wasn't sure if her nerves should reassure him or make him more anxious.

He considered initiating a conversation, but her scowl did nothing to encourage the idea. If she wanted to talk let her make the first move. He leaned back and sighed. Why couldn't they just get on with it?

Nosorova looked his way. "Did you put your affairs in order?"

He blinked. That was a hell of a thing to ask a man. "Should I have?"

"We are not summoned to receive His Majesty's compliments, not after the debacle at the docks. My only hope is that he'll show a little mercy and grant us swift deaths."

Yarik swallowed. "I was thinking more an official reprimand and maybe a demotion."

Her laugh held no humor. "The czar doesn't meet with people like us to offer reprimands."

The door to the waiting room opened and a bald man wearing a white uniform that strained to contain his bulk said, "You are called."

Yarik nodded and got to his feet. He and Nosorova followed the guard across a wide corridor. A set of double doors stood open and a rich white carpet showing not a speck of dirt led down a path lined with hundreds of hard, dark wooden chairs. Every chair held a man or woman wearing pure white dress clothes. Some showed a bit of gold at the neck or wrist, but most went unadorned.

At the end of the carpet on a raised dais, sat a golden throne. Two witches in shimmering white robes stood on either side of it. Further back along the walls various advisors and dignitaries stood, silent and watching. Of the czar he saw no sign.

The guard motioned them on with a nod. Yarik steeled himself and marched down the carpet. He looked neither left nor right. One of the individuals behind the throne caught his eye. She wore gray robes with white fur at the collar and a mask that resembled a dog or wolf. He'd never seen anything like it. Who in the world could she be?

They stopped at the end of the carpet fifteen feet from the throne. Yarik wanted to see what Nosorova was doing, but didn't dare shift his gaze.

Five minutes passed and he'd just begun to wonder how long they'd have to wait when a horn sounded followed by a deep voice. "His Imperial Majesty Roman Orlova, the Dragon Czar."

Yarik dropped to his knees and stared at the floor. He didn't even need to think. All children were taught how to react should they ever encounter the czar. It was drilled into them from their first day at school, even before that if their parents were smart.

A heavy tread sent vibrations through the floor then the throne creaked as if a great weight had settled into it.

"Rise," said a voice so deep it made Yarik's chest ache.

He scrambled to his feet and looked for the first time on his czar. It took Yarik a moment to wrap his mind around the being in front of him. The Dragon Czar wore no shirt, instead silver-white scales covered his massive torso from his stomach to his chin and down the backs of both arms. Yellow eyes with vertical pupils bore into Yarik. It wouldn't take much to imagine that gaze consuming his mind altogether.

Finally the piercing eyes turned to Nosorova. "I offer you one chance to explain why three of my White Witches are dead."

"Forgive me, my czar," Nosorova said. "The rebels had Death's Head bullets. They tore through my sisters' defenses like they were nothing. The only way we could have avoided what happened was to stay out of the field. Had we done that we chanced a reputation for cowardice. If the people cease to fear and respect us we risk chaos."

"Well said." The czar's lips peeled back, revealing needle-sharp teeth. "The rebels are worms. Our true enemy is the Court of Midnight. The vampires provided the bullets that killed my servants. They also slaughtered my soldiers when they attempted to apprehend the rebels who fled Anapa."

Yarik barely controlled his reaction. He'd heard nothing about any of this, though it certainly made sense. All the reports he'd read indicated the vampires were skilled in dark magic and all the items the rebels had used were of that type.

The czar's yellow eyes slid over to Yarik. "Does my revelation surprise you, Agent Yarik?"

"Only in so much as I'm surprised I didn't put the clues together myself. I know the Empire hasn't had good relations with our neighbors to the west and I doubt the Iron Lord of the East would stoop to working with humans."

"You're quite correct. In my generosity I've decided to spare you both. Clearly you were the victims of an outside conspiracy. Nosorova, you shall have a chance at revenge. When my army marches west, you will be at the vanguard, bringing your magic to bear against the undead."

Nosorova bowed. "I'm honored by the opportunity, Majesty."

"And you, Agent, will continue your pursuit of the rebels and my future witch."

Yarik couldn't speak for a moment. How was he supposed to hunt them down in the vampires' territory? Out loud he said, "As Your Majesty commands."

The czar's smile widened. "I see from your reaction you don't understand. My spies have learned the rebel's ultimate goal lies beyond the vampires' land. She's going to the Kingdom of the Isles. Other agents will be watching all the airports. The runaways will know this which leaves them with only one good option, the port of Calais. One of my allies will meet you there and provide manpower. Also, Hedon, Victor, come here."

Two bald men that could have been twins of the door guard stood up from the end of the front row of chairs. They had to be close to seven feet tall.

"Hedon and Victor are dragon-bloods adept at hiding their gifts. They will join you as bodyguards. I'm confident that the three of you will succeed."

Yarik was glad someone was confident since he sure wasn't. Taking two dragon-bloods into a country in the middle of a civil war to try and find one particular girl—what could possibly go wrong?

* * *

Anya watched in stunned silence as six humanoid shadows bore her mother's body away. They had to be vampires, but their forms wavered so that she couldn't get a clear look at them. She took a step to follow, but Lord Talon blocked her path.

"I fear where she's going the living can't follow."

"Where are they taking her?" Anya asked, her gaze never leaving the slowly shrinking procession.

"The Chamber of Shadows. It's where all new members of the court go to await their rebirth. Rest assured, she will never be alone."

"We need to get going," Fedor said. "More than half the journey remains."

"Can't we stay until my mother wakes up? She'll be worried about me."

"No time." Fedor scratched his beard and sighed. "We need to be in Calais in four weeks to meet our contact and make the trip to the Kingdom. There's no time to spare."

"We'll stay here," Yanni said. "Catch a ride back with our next supply ship."

"You are most welcome, Captain," Lord Talon said. He smiled at Anya. "I will be your guide until sunrise and will be happy to answer any questions you may have. My country is sparsely populated, but the natural beauty is something few mortals get to enjoy."

Anya smiled back. She found the pale lord far more pleasant than she'd expected when she first heard they were coming here. "I suppose you don't have a department of tourism."

He laughed a warm, hearty chuckle. "No, we're also extremely lacking in hotels."

At Lord Talon's whistle a black limo emerged from one of the warehouses. All the windows save the windshield had dark glass. It drove over to them and a man dressed in a black uniform climbed out. Given his skin tone and steady breathing she judged him human. The driver opened the back door and held it for them.

Fedor shook hands with Yanni and Jacob before joining Anya and Lord Talon in the limo. When the driver closed the door it was completely dark inside. A moment later a light in the roof burst to life, revealing a rich interior complete with gold drink service, refrigerator, and television.

The car lurched a little then smoothed out. She looked out the window, but it was so dark she couldn't make out much. Anya yawned. The craziness of the past hour had left her exhausted.

"May I offer you something to eat?" Lord Talon asked.

Her mouth watered at the thought of food then she remembered who was offering. "I'm not sure."

He laughed again. "I'm not offering a chalice of blood or whatever you imagine we enjoy here. While the population is small, thousands of humans live in this land and some of them work for us in various capacities. One of which is to cook for any mortal guests that might visit. I believe Esmerelda fixed shredded lamb sandwiches."

He opened the refrigerator, removed a sealed container, and handed it to her. Anya hesitantly opened it, to his apparent amusement. Inside she found three rolls wrapped in paper along with full water bottles. Anya handed a bottle and sandwich to Fedor. She looked for a long moment at the extra sandwich and water. Mom should have been there with her.

She sighed, took her meal, and dug in. The tender meat melted in her mouth and the spices tickled the back of her throat.

She was halfway through with her meal when she noticed Lord Talon had nothing for himself. "Aren't you hungry?"

He smiled and revealed his elongated eyeteeth. "I had a

large meal last night. I won't need to feed again for several days."

Her stomach twisted when he said "feed." For a few minutes she'd forgotten what he was. "I see."

She tried to return to her food, but found her appetite curdled. What had she consigned her mother to? Maybe it would have been better to let her pass on.

"I see you misunderstand again," Lord Talon said. "Only on the rarest occasions do we partake of human blood. Usually when our obnoxious neighbor to the east sends his butchers into the mountains to hunt down my sleeping brothers and sisters. No, we much prefer to hunt and feed on wild animals. I myself have acquired a taste for boar. Many times we don't even bother to kill the animal as we require only a liter or so of blood at a time. Most larger animals can sustain the loss with little ill effects."

Anya shook her head and took another bite. "So much of what we're taught is wrong. What's the point of having school if you're learning nonsense?"

"The Empire teaches what the czar wants you to know," Fedor said. He'd finished his dinner and was sipping the last of his water. "The resistance is a terrorist group, vampires are monsters that will kill you in an instant, the White Witches are loyal and devoted servants of the Empire. All lies that serve the government by turning its citizens against those who genuinely wish to help. It's disgusting."

That was the longest and most heartfelt speech Fedor had ever made. Clearly his hatred for the Empire was genuine. Anya yawned again. She understood the feeling. After everything that had happened she'd worked up a pretty good hate for it as well.

* * *

Fedor waited until Anya had fallen asleep to broach the subject of the rebellion. It didn't take long for the fear and stress to combine with a full stomach to put her lights out. He wasn't sure if she'd made the correct decision, having Sasha be turned, but it was her choice to make and Fedor had no intention of second guessing her. Having lost so much already, he understood her choice.

"She's a remarkable girl." Lord Talon pitched his voice low so as not to wake her. "I see why you chose her to be your representative to the outside world."

Fedor tore his gaze away from Anya and focused on the vampire. He would have liked to say the decision came out of some coldblooded planning, but the truth was, the moment Anya showed wizard potential, there was no question of letting the Empire have her.

"What will the czar do now?" Fedor asked.

Lord Talon bared a fang. "Roman will never let something he believes is his go. I fear once you leave my protection you will face more Imperial agents before your journey is through."

It jarred Fedor a moment to hear someone call the czar by his first name and without so much as an honorific. Of course, to an immortal like Lord Talon even the five-hundred-year-old Dragon Czar was little more than a child. A petulant one given to tantrums.

"Will he move against you and your people?" Fedor asked.

Lord Talon laughed, cold and humorless. "I hope he's so stupid. His hunters may slay an occasional vampire that gets careless and wanders too close to the border near dawn, but we'd slaughter his army in a single night, witches or no witches. No, I believe our war will remain cold."

Fedor nodded. That was The Manager's assessment as well. "Will you continue to send us weapons to use against the witches?"

"With great pleasure. What that creature does to those girls is an abomination. Freeing them from his control is a gift to the world as well as to the girls."

Fedor made no comment on Lord Talon's disgust given that what the czar did was almost exactly the same as the vampires themselves did to create new members of their family.

"You think me a hypocrite?" Lord Talon asked.

"Did you read my mind?"

"No need. I've been reading the expressions of mortals since before the coming of the elves. You control yourself better than most and the beard helps, but it's not enough to hide from me."

"I meant no offense."

"I know. The truth, my friend, is that we don't turn anyone unless they wish it. To do otherwise is the greatest crime in our society. Vampires have been staked out in the sun for that sin."

Fedor shuddered. "How long will it take to reach the border?"

Lord Talon shrugged. "A week I hope. This is a rough land now. I can make no promises."

No promises. That could have been the motto of this venture.

* * *

A nya sat up and rolled her shoulders. Sleeping on the seat of a car, even one as luxurious as Lord Talon's limo, wasn't the easiest on a person's neck. Across from her Fedor was sitting up and scratching his beard. Lord Talon sat beside him, silent and dark.

She looked out the window, but the sun hadn't risen yet and she couldn't see a thing beyond the faint glow of the head-lights. She eyed the refrigerator, but wasn't certain the protocol when asking a vampire lord for breakfast.

He must have noticed where she was looking as he smiled and said, "In an hour or so we'll reach a cabin where we can gas up the car and you two can get a meal."

"The sun will be up by then," Anya said. She'd been wrong about so many other things she didn't want to take anything for granted at this point. "Won't that be a problem for you?"

"In one sense it will, but this car is designed for trans-porting us day or night. The tinting on the windows is more than it seems. Dark magic has been mixed with the chemicals to filter out all the harmful effects of sunlight. As long as I remain inside I'll be able to sleep safely. I will be paralyzed and completely helpless until the sun sets again. It's an unfortunate side effect of my condition."

"What about garlic and crosses?" she asked.

He laughed. "Harmless, both of them. I love all the supersti-tions that you mortals have imagined for us. I especially like the one about running water. Why you would think a brook should pose an impenetrable barrier to us is beyond me."

"I suppose if humans have one thing in abundance it's imagination."

A shiver ran through Lord Talon. "Forgive me, my dear, but would you mind very much switching places with me?"

Anya got up and they switched spots. "Is that better?" she asked.

"Very much. The sun will rise in seconds. You two will be in good hands with Claus and I will see you in the evening." His form shivered again and dissolved into a black mist that disappeared under the seat cushion.

"What was that about?" Anya asked. "He said he'd be safe in the car."

"But we have to get out," Fedor said. "And when we do the sun will enter. I suspect there's a sealed compartment built under the seat for extra protection."

"Like a portable coffin." She grinned. It appeared some of the myths were true.

Fifteen minutes later the sun cleared the horizon and the limo pulled into a driveway. At the end of it waited a modest log cabin that would have been right at home in any village in the Empire. The limo pulled up beside the door and they climbed out as quickly as possible before slamming the door shut.

The driver joined them a moment later. "This is where we part company. Claus will refill the car and drive you during the day shift. I'm going in to get a bit of breakfast. Would you care to join me?"

Anya leapt at the offer and she and Fedor followed the driver inside. The interior of the building looked exactly like what you'd expect, three rooms done in rough timbers. Minimal decorations, an end table here, an old oil painting hanging there, all very basic and unremarkable.

"I hope you like eggs," the driver said. "Our pantry is pretty limited out here."

"Eggs sound great," Anya said. "But I need to find the bathroom."

"Down the hall to your right." The driver waved her toward a side hall.

Anya hurried away. At the end of the hall were two doors. Did he mean the right-hand door or that the hall itself was to her right? Anya's knees were knocking so she grabbed the handle of the right-hand door.

Inside she found a simple bedroom with a small wardrobe and dressing table. The closet door was open and light streamed out. Someone was obviously getting dressed in there. She started to close the door again, but she heard a voice from behind the closet door.

"The car just arrived," a male voice said. "I'll wait until noon to be sure. Don't worry, everything will be taken care of."

Not wanting to eavesdrop she finished shutting the door and went next door where she finally found the bathroom.

With a sigh of relief Anya went to rejoin the others in the kitchen. The driver stood at a propane stove scrambling eggs. Fedor sliced a loaf of dark bread and spread butter on it.

"Find the bathroom okay?" the driver asked.

"After a while. My first guess turned out to be someone's bedroom."

"Ah, was Claus ready?"

"He was in the closet, getting dressed I assume. I think he was talking to someone on his cellphone."

The driver frowned. "There's no cell service in the Land of the Night Princes."

"I really wish you hadn't heard that."

They all turned to find a man in a matching uniform standing in the doorway holding a pistol. Anya didn't know much about guns, but the barrel looked awfully big as she stood there staring down it.

"Claus? What are you doing?" The driver took a step toward him prompting Claus to shift his aim.

"I don't want to kill you, Tomas, but if you don't hold still I will."

"Have you lost your mind?" Tomas asked.

"He hasn't," Fedor answered for Claus. "I know that weapon. The mark seven is a favorite of the Imperial secret service. How long have you been undercover?"

"Too long. But now I'll win my way back into His Majesty's good graces. I'm going to return you two to the Empire, right after I kill Lord Talon."

Tomas took a step toward Claus. The spy cocked the hammer on his pistol. "I won't tell you again."

Tomas returned to his place. "You won't get away with this. The others will hunt you down long before you reach the Empire."

"They won't even know to look." Claus nodded to the hall. "Let's all go outside for a minute."

Anya made her way slowly down the hall and out into the yard, every step of the way imagining that gun going off and her journey ending. After all she'd survived, to think it would end up like this. Captured by an Imperial agent in the middle of nowhere.

They stopped a few feet from the limo. Claus pointed the gun at her. "Open the door."

Anya eased her way over and grasped the handle. She tugged it open and looked at her captor.

"Out of the way, girl, unless you want me to shoot through you."

She scrambled to Fedor's side. He put a big hand on her shoulder. "It'll be alright."

Anya wished she believed him.

The pistol boomed and a bullet pinged off the base of the seat.

Tomas laughed. "The secure chamber is made of half-inch-thick steel. You'll need something a hell of a lot stronger than that forty-five to get through it."

Claus snarled and pointed the pistol at Anya again. "Open the seat top."

"How?"

"I don't know. There's got to be a catch or something. Feel around."

"I don—"

"Now!"

Anya flinched at his shout. She had to think of something. Slowly she walked to the limo and climbed inside. The underside of the seat was smooth, no catch, no button, no nothing. Lord Talon had simply dissolved and vanished. Perhaps that was the only way in or out. If she were a vampire she wouldn't want a hiding place anyone could access just by pushing a button.

"Hurry up!" Claus shouted.

"I'm trying." She refused to give in to the tears gathering in the corners of her eyes.

"Don't yell at her," Fedor said. "She's been through enough."

Anya looked up from her futile search to find Fedor confronting the spy. Claus had the pistol jammed into his stomach.

Oh god, he was going to shoot Fedor. Anya would be all alone then. She didn't think, she just screamed, "I found it!"

Claus turned her way and the moment he did Fedor grabbed his wrist and twisted.

The pistol went off, but missed him.

Claus roared and the two men struggled back and forth. The gun wavered, pointing every which way.

Tomas lunged into the scrum, trying to help Fedor. They fell in a heap and rolled around, grunting and punching at each other.

The gun went off again and Tomas screamed.

Claus got free of Fedor who yelled, "Close the door!"

Anya grabbed the handle, yanked it shut, and flipped the lock. She was safe, but Fedor was alone out there with the spy. What should she do? What could she do?

"Open the door, girl. Open it or I'll kill your friend."

"Don't do it, Anya," Fedor said. "Stay in there until dark. Lord Talon will get you to safety."

Claus struck Fedor in the side of the head with his pistol, staggering the big man. "Shut up!"

Anya didn't know what to do. If she opened the door there was no doubt in her mind that both of them would end up dead, whether now or back home was the only question. If she didn't open up Claus would kill Fedor. What should she do?

Fear and uncertainty froze her. She looked around for inspiration, but neither the fancy interior of the limo or the log cabin outside provided any. Outside Tomas dragged himself toward the car.

What was he up to?

The half-dead driver grabbed Claus by the ankle.

When the spy looked down Fedor lunged toward him. He grabbed the barrel of the gun and wrenched it to the side.

Claus screamed when his index finger tore off. Fedor drew back and clobbered Claus in the temple with the pistol grip. He went down like a ton of bricks.

* * *

Fedor ripped open Tomas's blood-soaked shirt and tossed it aside. Anya winced when she saw the damage the bullet had done. All they'd been able to find was a simple first-aid kit in the cabin kitchen. She seriously doubted the two small painkillers they'd given him would make much of a difference.

Once the spy was bound and secure Fedor had carried the wounded driver inside and laid him on the bed. Anya fluttered around, alternating from wanting to help to wanting to throw up. Unfortunately neither she nor Fedor had much, if any, training as healers. God, there was so much she didn't know. She was completely useless.

Fedor packed gauze into the wound and bound it in place with strips of cloth. He straightened up and sighed. "I can do nothing more for him. Perhaps when he wakes Lord Talon will have a plan."

Anya hoped someone had a plan because theirs was falling apart in a hurry. "What should we do? It's got to be at least ten hours until sunset."

"We're going to tear Claus's room apart and see what we come up with. I doubt he'd be so stupid as to leave documents lying around, but maybe we can find whatever he used to contact the Empire."

They left the softly moaning Tomas to suffer in peace and made the short walk over to Claus's room. Nothing had changed since Anya entered by mistake. Had that only been half an hour ago? It felt like days.

She went straight to the closet. The inside looked ordinary enough. Two uniforms hung from a bar, a pair of black shoes rested on the floor. There was a shelf up above, but it was empty. She reached up and felt around, just in case something was hidden toward the back. No dice. That would have been too easy anyway.

To her left Fedor was emptying the drawers of a chest on the floor. Nothing but linens and towels. She'd seen a few spy movies over the years. Usually the agent would hide his gear in a secret compartment.

Anya tapped the back wall of the closet and listened. Halfway across it still sounded pretty solid. She reached the far side and it *still* sounded solid. So much for that.

"The dresser's a bust," Fedor said. "Help me flip the bed."

Anya left her fruitless search of the closet and joined him. Together they flipped the mattress over on its side then let it fall to the floor. Nothing underneath. The box spring got the same treatment, joining the mattress on the floor revealing the bare floor.

Fedor sighed. "This is getting us nowhere. Where could he have hidden his phone?"

"Was it even a phone?" Anya asked. "Tomas said there was no cell service here."

Fedor slapped his forehead. "Of course not. The witches must have provided him with a communication device."

He rushed over to the pile of linens and pawed through them, finally coming up with a brass hand mirror. "I'll wager this is it. I've seen similar items taken from dead spies. Pity I don't know how to make it work."

"Would you really want to talk to whoever was liable to answer?"

"Good point. Let's get a bite to eat. We can't do anything else until dark."

* * *

A nya and Fedor stood together facing the limo as the sun sank below the horizon. The instant it vanished a black mist gathered in the air and solidified into the pale figure of Lord Talon.

"My friends, I am so sorry. I hadn't the slightest idea we had a rat in our midst. He must have turned after joining my service as I vet all my employees most thoroughly."

"How can you know what happened?" Anya asked. "I thought you were unconscious inside your coffin."

"Not unconscious, just unable to move. I heard everything that happened. How fares Tomas?"

"Not good," Fedor said. "We did what we could, but it didn't amount to much."

"There is very little violence in my land so we don't stock much in the way of medical supplies at these cabins. Until today I would have said there was no need."

"You can do something for him though, right?" Anya asked.

Lord Talon's smile was bleak. "We shall see."

The vampire led the way inside and went straight to the bedroom where Tomas lay, unconscious, on the bed. Lord Talon drew in a sharp breath. "It's worse than I feared."

"You can't help him?" What had Anya expected? He couldn't heal her mother, why would he be able to do something for Tomas? The shock must have broken her mind.

"No. As far as I know there isn't a single light magic healer in the entire country." Lord Talon leaned closer to Tomas. "Wake, my friend. I must ask you something."

Tomas's eyes struggled open. "My lord, I'm sorry. I had no idea about Claus. Forgive me."

"Have no fear on that count, Tomas. He slipped under my

nose as well. For your service I would offer you entry into the Court of Midnight."

Tomas gave a weak shake of his head. "No, my lord. Thank you, but I am not worthy of such a gift."

"You understand that without my blessing you will die?"

"Yes, my lord. Will you send word to my wife and tell her I died well?"

"I will tell her myself. Rest now. I will stay until the Endless Night takes you."

Tomas's eyes closed and Lord Talon held his hand. Tears streamed down Anya's face. Each breath Tomas took grew ever more shallow, until at last he breathed no more.

"Why didn't he take the offer?" Anya asked. "He could have gone on living, sort of."

"His wife," Fedor said. "Eternal life would mean watching her grow old and die before his eyes. I couldn't have faced it either."

"You are correct." Lord Talon rose, barely contained fury causing his body to tremble. "I had forgotten Tomas was married. If I'd recalled I never would have offered him the gift. Where is Claus? He has much to answer for."

"We left him tied up in the kitchen," Fedor said. "Figured you'd want to talk to him when you woke up."

Lord Talon's eyes flashed red. "He will talk, of that you may be sure."

Anya swallowed the sudden lump in her throat as they followed the vampire into the kitchen. In that moment he appeared every bit the monster she'd first believed him to be. Claus was slumped against the stove where they'd left him. Blood trickled down his cheek from the wound on his head.

Lord Talon grabbed him by the throat and lifted him off the floor like he was a child. "Wake up, you miserable wretch."

When Claus didn't react at once Lord Talon shook him until his teeth rattled.

Anya hurried over to the sink and drew a cup of ice-cold water. "Lord Talon, if I may?"

He looked at her with eyes that glowed like coals in a stove. He dropped Claus to the floor. "Go ahead."

Anya tossed the water in his face and Claus sat up sputtering. He spotted Lord Talon and shrank back against the cabinets.

"Please, my lord, show mercy."

"The same mercy you would have shown me and my guests? The same mercy you showed Tomas? Is that the mercy you plead for?"

"No, I only sought a better life. The czar would have rewarded me greatly. Blame him, not me."

"Oh, I do. I blame the dragon pig, but that doesn't absolve you of your guilt and you're here in front of me while he is far away. I am not without mercy. Tell me everything your czar has planned and I will grant you the mercy of a quick death. In all honesty it would please me greatly if you make me beat the information out of you."

"I don't know much, I'm a nobody. I've been watching this miserable shack for years with nothing to report to my superiors. When you all showed up I thought I'd been given the biggest break of my life. The order was sent out to all foreign agents to be on the lookout for a blond girl traveling with a large bearded man and an older woman. They were to be returned to the Empire for punishment. We had permission to kill the man and woman, but His Majesty wanted the girl alive."

"What else?" Lord Talon asked.

"That's all, I swear." The spy trembled and scrunched down

into himself. If he hadn't just admitted to being willing to kill Fedor and her mother Anya might have felt bad for him. As it was she had nothing but loathing.

Lord Talon snatched him off the floor and stared into his eyes. Claus went stiff then limp.

After a moment Lord Talon said, "He's telling the truth. He really is a worthless worm. You may not want to watch this."

Anya stood straight. "He would see me a slave of the czar and my mother dead. Whatever punishment you give him, I will witness."

Lord Talon's faint smile revealed a hint of his right fang. "You have steel in you, girl. I fear you'll need all of it and then some. Very well."

He opened his mouth and the fangs grew from one inch to four. Quick as a blink he used those fangs to tear Claus's throat out. Anya winced, but refused to look away. The bastard deserved what he got.

Blood gushed and Lord Talon gulped it down. When the flow stopped he went to the door and tossed the body out into the backyard.

Power burst from Lord Talon and the blood that had covered his face and clothes vanished. "The wolves will make short work of that trash. We must be on our way if you're to make your destination on time. I will drive you myself tonight and tomorrow we'll pick up a new chauffeur. I will assure myself of his loyalty before leaving you with him. This will not happen again. I swear it."

Anya found she believed every word he said. She certainly wouldn't want to be the one that betrayed him next.

* * *

After three days and nights of driving through winding mountain roads, some of which looked barely wide enough for the limo, much less two cars, they finally reached civilization. The sun had just set and Lord Talon emerged from his daily rest when the jutting towers of the city appeared in the side window. From a distance the dark city appeared perfect. Skyscrapers pierced the sky, far higher than anything she'd seen at home. But where were the lights?

They made a sharp turn off the dirt road they'd been following and onto a proper paved street. Derelict, rusty cars sat on the edge of the road. From the look of them they'd been waiting there for a long time.

Half an hour later they reached the outskirts of the city. Up close it was every bit as dark as she'd thought. No people moved around and the buildings looked deserted.

"What happened here?" Anya asked.

"The people fled," Lord Talon said. "No one has lived in the cities of my land for a long time."

"Why?"

He turned to look out the window, a melancholy frown crinkling his brow. "The elves came."

Anya shivered. How many horror stories began with that line?

"It was two years into the invasion and they'd just finished destroying Budapest when they turned their sights south. The humans fought bravely, but wizards had never been common in this area and NATO's magical brigade had more important countries to defend. Not that they were much use there either. Many of my people argued that we should stay out of the fight, leave the humans to their own devices. They'd been hunting us for centuries, many said. See how they like being the prey."

Anya nodded. It wouldn't be easy to convince anyone to fight for their enemies.

"I argued that when the elves finished with the humans they'd turn their magic on us. Those who agreed with me attacked. It turned out that the elves were weak against our powers and over the course of a month of nights we drove them out. We also revealed our numbers and powers to the humans. They were as afraid of us as of the elves. Most of the population packed up and left. After the war I made it known that any that wished to return would be safe, but few did. My land is a hollow shell, dotted with empty cities."

"I'm sorry. You seem nice enough to me."

Fedor chuckled and Lord Talon shrugged before smiling. "Maybe one day the people will return. I no longer care."

"They'll probably return with an army armed with stakes and swords," Fedor said.

Lord Talon bared his fangs. "We would not take kindly to that sort of return."

Anya shivered, glad once again that the vampire was on her side.

It took eight days to travel from one side of the territory to the other, but at last they stopped a hundred feet from a border crossing manned by ten men armed with machine guns. The crossing was lit up by a handful of bright sodium lights and a modest-sized building sat off to one side of the road.

None of the soldiers raised their weapon, but from the way they fidgeted Anya could tell they were nervous. Probably because they knew who, or more accurately what, was in the limo.

Lord Talon must have noticed her eyeing the soldiers because he reached out and patted her hand. His fingers were ice cold. "Don't worry, there's a protocol for this sort of thing.

When their commander appears we'll get out and take care of the transfer."

He reached under his shirt, pulled out a gold-inlayed cross with a red crystal in the center, and lifted it over his head. "Here. This is your token of safe passage. Wear this and you can travel anywhere in my land without fear. As I said, any time you wish to visit your mother you are welcome."

Anya slipped the cross over her head and tucked it out of sight. Before she could thank him Lord Talon said, "Here he comes."

The three of them piled out of the limo and went to meet a middle-aged man in a brown uniform sporting over a dozen ribbons. Lord Talon took the lead and the two men stopped a few feet apart.

"Lord Talon." The soldier bowed.

"Major. I trust all is well in Germany?"

The major blew out a sigh through his thick mustache. "As well as can be expected with a civil war raging to our west. As always the Kaiser appreciates you keeping things peaceful on your side of the border."

Lord Talon chuckled. "Given that the entire population of my nation is less than one of your smaller cities, keeping the peace isn't difficult. May I introduce my guests? Anya and Fedor."

"I was told to expect three. Where's the woman?"

Anya flinched and Fedor gave her a reassuring squeeze on the shoulder.

"Alas," Lord Talon said. "She had an unfortunate encounter with the Imperial navy. The young lady's mother will be my guest for the foreseeable future."

The major lowered his gaze. "My apologies and condolences. I meant no insult, miss."

Anya nodded. "It's okay. There's no way you could have known. Thank you for letting us pass through your country."

His face turned into a mass of wrinkles when he smiled. "Not at all. Lord Talon so seldom asks for a favor, granting it is the least we can do on the rare occasions he does. Shall we go? I'm sure you're anxious to continue your journey."

The only thing Anya was anxious to do was sleep in a real bed, but she bowed to Lord Talon. "Thank you for everything. Please tell my mother I love her."

He smiled again. "I will. And as I said, feel free to visit again any time."

The vampire lord took his leave and she and Fedor followed the major across the border into Germany. One more leg of their journey complete. Now all they had to do was cross a war-torn land and make it to the Kingdom of the Isles in one piece. Now that they were more than halfway there it actually felt possible.

7

A LAND AT WAR

I t wouldn't take much, Yarik decided, to truly despise Calais. From his perch in one of the towers of the True Face of God cult's church he could look out over the wretched, burned-out city. Fire did more to illuminate the night than electricity since the nearby power station was blown up over a year ago. The religious nuts controlled three-quarters of the place including the waterfront. Which was good since that was almost certainly where the girl would try and make her escape.

A faint hint of char reached him. He'd been in the city for five days and there was always something burning. On a good day it was an abandoned building. On a bad one it was some poor bastard that did something the inquisitors didn't approve of. And that was a long list that occasionally changed if the inquisitor in question didn't like your looks.

Why in the world did the czar agree to work with these madmen? Not that he'd ever say anything against the czar, may he rule forever, but the Empire had basically outlawed

142

the worship of anything but the czar himself, so a religious cult didn't seem like the most likely ally for him. Granted they did rule all of what used to be Spain and Portugal and was now called the Blessed Realm. Blessed for the priests maybe, but he doubted the regular people living there were so happy.

Yarik flicked a speck of ash off his suit coat. If Anya was coming he wished she'd hurry up and get here so he could capture her and go home.

The tread of a heavy boot came from the staircase behind him. Yarik turned to find Hedon or was it Victor, well one of the dragon-bloods at any rate, standing in the hatch.

"What?"

"There's a spy on the communicator, Agent. She has news of the target."

At last. "Let's go."

Yarik followed the dragon-blood down three flights of steps to the hall. The passage to the right led to the cathedral. They turned left to the small prayer chamber the priests had delegated for their use. It wasn't much bigger than Yarik's office at home. For three big men it made for a tight and smelly fit.

The final member of their little group waited inside holding a small, bronze-handled mirror. A female face framed by blond hair filled the glass.

Yarik took the communicator. "You have news?"

"Yes, Agent. The target was spotted on the road to Paris. We almost overlooked her since only the girl and the man were present. My subordinate has been following them from a distance and there's no sign of the mother."

"No matter. She was never a priority. What assets do we have in Paris?"

"Minimal, I'm afraid. Just me and three others. Our cell was put in place to spy not carry out a snatch and run."

"That's fine, just keep an eye on them. I'll be there with reinforcements by morning. Well done."

"Zolta. I'd appreciate it if you remembered my name in your final report."

"Of course. If this goes well I'll put in a good word for you. Maybe get you promoted out of this toilet."

Zolta nodded and the connection went dead. Yarik put the communicator on the little table in the center of the room and grinned. "Get ready to move. We've got a lock on the target."

Hedon and Victor smiled, displaying far too many pointy teeth. It was so easy to forget they weren't fully human.

"How are we going to travel?" one of them asked.

"We'll requisition a car from our…Which one are you?"

"Hedon, sir."

Yarik reached into his coat pocket and pulled out a blue ballpoint pen. "Bend down."

Hedon did as he said and Yarik drew a blue H on his forehead. Nothing ostentatious, just a little mark below his hairline, if he'd had hair, so Yarik wouldn't be constantly wondering which was which.

"There. Now, we'll get a car from the priests. They have to have something. If worst comes to worst we can use the pickup they brought us here in. Pack up our stuff. I'll go see Father Gabriele."

He left the dragon-bloods to their task. Shouldn't take long since they each only brought a single bag. At the end of the hall a set of heavy oak double doors led to the church cathedral. Yarik shoved them open and strode inside. The pews were empty, but Father Gabriele stood in front of the altar, hands clasped in prayer. He dressed in an all-black priest's outfit. A gold cross hung down on his chest.

The priest turned and threw his hands to the sky. "Welcome, brother. Have you come to pray? The True Face of God welcomes all who embrace him, even a damned heathen like you."

"Not today, Father," Yarik said. "One of our assets spotted the target this afternoon. She's in Paris and we need transport."

"No problem, no problem. We have a bus that will serve the cause admirably. Twenty of my men will lend a hand. Paris is a big place after all. They will find the godless witch and set her on the proper course. Fire and steel, Agent. Fire and steel can cleanse even the most godless and turn them to light."

"The czar wants her intact and undamaged. If that's going to be a problem, me and my men can manage on our own."

"No, no! The church honors our agreements. The Archbishop said you are to be afforded whatever aid you require and we shall obey. Obedience, Agent, is also a supreme duty in the church."

Well, that was one thing the church and the Empire had in common. "Great. Where's the bus? We'll meet your men outside."

"Around back. We will join you shortly."

"We?"

"Yes, I will come along to lead my troops in the holy crusade. The vile witch will not escape us, rest assured."

Of all the things Yarik felt upon learning that Father Gabriele would be joining them, assurance was at the bottom of the list.

* * *

Anya had read many books, both fiction and nonfiction, set in Paris. When the little two-door car the German army had donated for their journey pulled into the outskirts of the city it was instantly clear none of those books had been updated in a while. The first and most obvious thing was the City of Lights wasn't very well lit. In fact, other than their headlights Anya hadn't seen a single electric light. Fire, on the other hand, was prevalent.

Fedor hit a deep pothole, jarring her and making her wish they hadn't left Germany. That portion of the trip had easily been the most pleasant. From one side of the country to the other they had a military escort. The roads were smooth and no one tried to kill them. The people had been kind and generous, the food delicious, and the beds she slept in each of their three nights in the country soft and warm.

She sighed. Maybe it would be best to forget about Germany. Until they reached the Kingdom of the Isles comfort was going to be a luxury.

"Where are we going?" Anya asked.

"Free French Army safe house." Fedor kept his eyes on the road. "The resistance leadership made a deal with them to help with the journey in exchange for Kingdom weapons. We get one night of safety and sleep then we head for Calais in the morning."

Anya yawned. Sleep sounded good. Her schedule was all messed up after the time they spent in the Land of the Night Princes. She hoped her mom was adjusting to her new life.

The street ran through a slum filled with sagging tenements and litter-choked alleys. The world beyond their headlights should have been filled with people, but all she saw was junk and ruin. Could this be the same city she'd read about? It didn't seem possible.

"What happened here?" Anya asked.

"War. When the Blessed Army invaded they weren't gentle. I've read estimates that a third of the population has been killed and another third displaced. Everyone that could, fled the cities. It's easier to survive in the country. The only people in the city now are soldiers and looters."

"How do you know so much? They didn't teach us any of this in school."

"No reason they would. As for me, I told you, we've been planning this for a while. I did research on every leg of the trip, even spoke to a member of the French army. It was an enlightening conversation. Depressing as hell, but enlightening."

Fedor swerved around a crater. "Keep your eyes open for a subway entrance. The army is using the underground to move around and store supplies."

Great, she'd get to spend the night in a dank, dark hole surrounded by sweaty, smelly soldiers. Sometimes, not often, but sometimes, she wondered if being a White Witch would really be worse than this.

The car swerved again and Fedor pulled into an alley. He turned it off and pulled out the keys. A hundred feet off the street a set of steps descended to the underground.

Anya climbed out, then walked over, and started down the stairs. At the bottom a set of heavy steel bars stopped them cold. Beyond the bars a warm yellow light revealed gray tiles and a row of rectangular columns.

A man in a green uniform stepped into view. He had a machine gun pointed at Fedor's chest. "You've got the wrong station, my friend."

"No," Fedor said. "General de Gaulle sent us."

The soldier put his rifle up and grinned. "Why didn't you say so in the first place? We've been expecting you for a few days now. Where have you been?"

"We ran into a few unexpected delays. You know how it is when you're traveling." Fedor eyed the bars. "You want to let us in? I'm feeling a little exposed out here."

The soldier smacked a hand into his forehead. "But of course. Where is my head? No doubt the young beauty with you has me distracted."

He walked back to where he came from and a moment later the bars rose into the ceiling. Fedor led the way in. Once they were clear the bars came crashing down.

The guard left his weapon leaning against the wall and rejoined them.

"I'm Pierre." He took Anya's hand and kissed the back of it. Now that she saw him clearly she realized he wasn't much older than her. "Welcome to the Legion."

"I'm Anya, nice to meet you. Thanks for letting us stay here."

He released her and gave a negligent wave of his hand. "Not at all. The weapons that were provided have allowed us to nearly reclaim the city. When the next shipment arrives we'll push the bastards out of France altogether. Just wait."

She smiled. "I'm sure you will."

Fedor cleared his throat. "Your commander is expecting us."

"Of course, of course. Forgive me. It's been far too long since I had a beautiful woman to talk to. I got carried away. You see the red arrows?"

Anya looked where he pointed and sure enough a red arrow was painted on the station wall. It almost glowed in the light of the kerosene lanterns hanging from the ceiling. Fedor grunted an acknowledgment.

"Just follow them. Be sure to ignore the yellow and blue ones though, they'll lead you into trouble."

Fedor nodded. "Thanks. Ready?"

"Yes," Anya said. "I fear I might fall asleep on my feet."

They trudged down the platform, down a set of steps, and along the rails for what seemed like miles, but was probably only a few hundred yards. The tunnel opened into a round cavern. Four more lines converged on the spot. All around fire burned and men in uniforms either sat beside them or tended bubbling pots. Two dozen tents had been set up against the walls.

Hard, hostile eyes looked up as they entered. Anya huddled closer to Fedor. This lot seemed far less friendly than the boy at the entrance. You'd have thought that, having made it past the guard, everyone would know they weren't enemies.

"Where's your commander?" Fedor asked.

"Here." A tall, wiry man with a white mustache emerged from one of the tents. "Are you the friends of de Gaulle?"

"We are." Fedor stepped in front of her and held out his hand.

The commander shook it and said, "It's about time. I feared you might not make it and then we wouldn't get our second shipment. But you're here now, that's what's important. Are you hungry? We have a variety of stews cooking."

Anya yawned and Fedor said, "Perhaps you could show us to our tent? My companion is tired."

"Certainly, follow me." He led them to a tent that looked like more patch than canvas. "Here you are. Sleep well."

The rickety cot inside was the most welcoming sight Anya

had seen in a long time. She collapsed into it and was asleep in seconds.

* * *

Yarik's legs were shaking when he climbed down out of the yellow bus. Father Gabriele must have been anxious to meet his god given the way he drove down the potholed highway that led from Calais to Paris. On more than one occasion Yarik was certain they tipped over on just one set of wheels. While the ride hadn't been anyone's idea of smooth, at least they arrived before sunrise. The hours just before dawn were always the best time to attack.

Before him Paris sprawled, a ruined shell of its former glory. Victor, Hedon, and the priest joined him out in the street. The twenty holy warriors Gabriele had brought with him remained in their seats, heads bowed in prayer. They'd been like that since the bus pulled out of the church parking lot. They must have ridden with Father Gabriele before.

"The communicator?" Yarik said.

Victor dug the bronze mirror out of his pack and handed it to him. Yarik focused on Zolta and five seconds later her face appeared.

"We're here, at the northern edge of the city," Yarik said.

"Your target is in the subway system. She and her guardian have made contact with the French army. I have a man watching the entrance they used."

Zolta gave him an address and Yarik said, "We'll be there as soon as we can."

She vanished from the mirror and Yarik handed it to Victor.

"Vile magic," Father Gabriele said. "You should bathe your

hands in holy water to cleanse the taint. I have some in the bus."

"That's generous of you, Father, but we don't have time just now. Did you hear our conversation?"

"Yes, I know the area she mentioned. It is fortunate they've found their way to the frogs. We shall roast them all in their holes and send their blasphemous souls to hell."

"I don't care what you do with the soldiers, but I need the girl alive." Given the priest's excessive fascination with fire, Yarik thought it best to keep reminding him this was a capture mission, not a kill mission.

They got back on the bus and the priest eased them into motion. It took most of half an hour to cross the burned-out city. Finally, Gabriele parked and opened the door.

"The street your spy mentioned is a block over. I thought it prudent to approach on foot."

Yarik nodded. He wouldn't have thought the zealous priest would have planned that far ahead. Never complain when the universe gives you a gift, his mother always said, lest it decide to take it back.

He studied the street ahead of them. It was too dark to make out the spy, but he did spot the subway entrance. Yarik turned to Hedon. "Do you see Zolta's man?"

The dragon-blood squinted and his eyes glowed with a faint yellow light. "I have him, he's almost directly opposite us in an alley overlooking the entrance."

Yarik took out a penlight from the inside of his jacket and flashed a sequence at the spy. A few seconds later a reply came: all clear. Good, they were free to attack. He flashed another message, freeing the spy from his task. Whatever happened now, his work was done. A single flash of acknowledgement and Yarik assumed the spy was gone.

"The situation hasn't changed," Yarik said. "Let's go get her."

Father Gabriele was busy blessing his men who stood with their heads bowed. Yarik's jaw clenched. If some overzealous holy warrior killed Anya he'd skin Gabriele alive.

The priest said, "Amen. We're ready, Agent."

The holy warriors raised their machine guns and Yarik led them toward the subway entrance. The group made far too much noise in the quiet night. *Please let the enemy be half asleep.* The group stopped at the top of the steps. At the bottom the entrance was sealed with heavy iron bars.

One of the soldiers pulled a grenade and reached for the pin. Yarik grabbed him. If they set off an explosion the girl would be gone before they ever reached the army camp. They needed to get in quietly. Fortunately they had just the men for the job.

Yarik clapped both the dragon-bloods on the shoulder. "You're up. Get us in there."

A magical glow surrounded both men. Talons sprouted from their fingers, scales ran down their arms and though he couldn't see, Yarik assumed their legs and chests as well. Their eyes turned yellow and began to glow.

Hedon and Victor marched down the steps.

A young man appeared in front of the bars on the other side. He rubbed his eyes and yawned. "Who goes—"

Hedon's arm shot through the bars, grabbed the kid by the throat, and crushed his neck. Together the two dragon-bloods grabbed the bars and heaved them up into a slot in the ceiling. The steel clattered, but not horribly.

Father Gabriele grabbed Yarik and spun him around. "You didn't say you fought with demons. How can noble servants of God fight beside such monstrosities?"

"Hedon and Victor are dragon-blooded, not demons. Their

powers are a gift from the czar himself. You don't mind taking weapons and money from our master, but you complain when his most-favored warriors come to fight beside you? Perhaps I should recommend to the czar that he find more reasonable allies."

"No need for that," the priest said. "A simple misunderstanding, you see. Let us go forth and slaughter the heathens."

Gabriele led his forces down the steps, careful not to touch Hedon or Victor. Yarik followed then paused beside his companions. "Let them worry about the French. Keep your eyes peeled for the girl. Once we find her we can leave this stinking dump."

The dragon-bloods flashed their fangs, he pulled his revolver, and the three of them set off after the holy warriors. The tunnel was lit by intermittent lanterns that barely kept Yarik from stumbling in the dark. On the plus side he spotted the glow from the French base three seconds before the first grenade went off.

Shouts and machine-gun fire echoed up the tunnel. Yarik let Hedon and Victor take the lead. Unless the enemy had heavy weapons, their scales would protect them from stray bullets. At the end of the tunnel they reached a round chamber filled with tents, many of them now on fire.

People ran and screamed and shot each other. It was everything he hated about war compressed in a tiny area. Hedon grunted when a bullet bounced off his chest.

A man in a green uniform came running at them with nothing but a long knife. Victor caught him by the wrist and throat then pulled. The soldier's arm went one way and his head the other.

Yarik ignored the quickly spreading pool of blood and tried

to pick a single girl out of the chaos. It was harder than he expected.

"Sir, in the back, near the left-most tunnel," Hedon said.

He spotted a flash of blond hair and pale skin. That was good enough for Yarik. "After her."

* * *

Anya sat straight up in the hard cot the French officer had provided for her. For half a second she stared around the dark tent and tried to figure out what had woken her. An explosion shook the canvas. The crack of automatic weapons filled the air.

What was going on? It sounded like a war out there.

The flap of her tent opened and Fedor stepped inside, his lantern making her squint. "We're under attack. Get dressed, it's time to go."

Anya scrambled over to the edge of the cot. All she needed to do was put on her socks and shoes. As she tugged them on she asked, "Who's attacking us?"

"The zealots I assume. I didn't stop to ask. Hurry."

She laced up her second boot and stood up. "I'm ready."

Fedor handed her a small automatic pistol. "Now you're ready. Remember what I taught you on the train. It's loaded and ready. Don't hesitate to use it if you need to."

He took her hand and they stepped out into Hell.

Tents were burning.

Men screamed as they died.

In the fire and madness she couldn't tell friend from foe.

Fedor tugged her toward the end of the chamber farthest from the fighting. They angled toward one of the tunnels that ran deeper into the subway system.

"Do you know where we're going?" Anya asked.

"Yeah, away from the people trying to kill us. Wherever this goes it's got to be better than staying back there."

She had no argument for that. They ran by the light of his lantern. The tracks had been torn up, but the wooden ties remained to try and trip them. It took all her concentration to stay upright.

Soon tumbled-down chunks of rock mixed with the timbers, turning the tunnel into an obstacle course. They slowed from a run to a quick walk to a shuffling trudge as the chunks of masonry grew ever larger.

"What happened down here?" Anya asked as she slipped between a pair of boulders as tall as she was.

Fedor grunted when he forced his bulk between the rocks. "The elves collapsed most of the tunnels during the war. Some got dug out, most didn't. The locals decided it was safer to travel on surface roads so no one bothered to finish the work."

She swung her leg over a waist-high stone, suddenly glad for the sturdy trousers and shirt she got on the boat. "You mean we have to climb over this rubble because the government got sick of cleaning the tunnels?"

"Basically." Fedor stopped and cocked his head.

"What?"

"Thought I heard something."

Anya held her breath and listened. After a few seconds she heard something scraping on stone followed by the crunch of boots on gravel. Someone was after them.

She grabbed Fedor's sleeve. "What are we going to do?"

"Keep calm, keep quiet, and keep moving," Fedor whispered. "We've got to be close to a street access."

Anya nodded and pushed on, moving as fast as she could

through the rubble. Please, let there be no real cave-ins. If they came to a dead end they'd really be in trouble.

No sooner had the thought crossed her mind than they reached a heap of rubble that reached just short of the ceiling fifteen feet over her head. There was a gap, but it would be a tight squeeze for her. How Fedor would fit she had no idea.

They eyed the pile and Fedor growled. "Let's get you up there."

"What about you?" Terror raced through Anya at the thought of traveling through the tunnels on her own. She didn't know where they were going, who they were meeting, none of it.

"I'll manage. If we get separated make for the Eiffel Tower Memorial."

"Where is that?"

"Near the city center. Just head north, you'll find signs pointing to it."

Fedor laced his fingers together and she put her foot in the stirrup. He heaved and she grabbed a protruding stone. Between them she got to the top and wriggled through the gap. On the other side it was pitch black, the only light coming from the gap and Fedor's lantern.

She stood in the dark, trembling and trying not to imagine what might be hiding in the tunnel. Spiders, rats, did snakes live in tunnels? Probably, if there were rats to eat.

Her skin crawled and she rubbed her arms. It was all in her head. They hadn't seen so much as a mouse since they'd been down here. There was no reason to think all the awful things were just waiting on this side of the rockfall, though they probably were.

"Catch!" She looked up just in time to grab the lantern

when Fedor lowered it down to her. He was halfway through the opening and wriggling for all he was worth.

Anya held the lantern up. *Hurry, hurry!*

One leg popped out then the other. He braced his feet and pushed.

"Ah!" Fedor came loose and tumbled down the slope.

Anya rushed over. Blood covered his right arm from an ugly gash in his bicep. She tore the sleeve of her shirt and tied it around the cut. He grunted when she tightened it.

"What happened?" Anya asked.

"Got stuck on a piece of rebar. We need to get going. Just before I got free I saw a light coming behind us. I couldn't tell who it was and I don't want to find out."

Anya seconded that motion and they were off. Beyond the rockfall the tunnel smoothed out and they set a brisker pace. Unfortunately there was nothing ahead of them but more tunnel. How far were they going to have to go to get out of here?

A little ways further she got her answer in the form of a set of rusty iron rungs hammered into the side of the tunnel. When she raised the lantern she saw there was a hatch or something in the ceiling.

Fedor looked up and frowned. "Emergency hatch. Probably rusted solid."

"Do we keep going?"

He looked up the tunnel and frowned. "Let's try it. I'd like to get out of here if we can."

"Me too."

He climbed up, grasped the mechanism, and twisted. The shriek of metal on metal hurt Anya's ears, but ever so slowly the release wheel turned. When the bolts had fully withdrawn Fedor put his shoulder against the hatch and pushed. It rose six inches, then a foot, then the rung Fedor was standing on snapped and he came crashing down to the tunnel floor.

"Are you okay?" Anya asked.

He muttered curses as he got up and brushed himself off. "Fine. Get on up there. I'll be right behind you."

He didn't have to tell her twice. Anya scrambled up the ladder and squeezed out the gap. She spun around as Fedor climbed up behind her. He put his shoulder to the hatch again and shoved.

A second rung broke and he fell once more to the tunnel floor. He looked up at her. "Go. I'll catch up."

Her stomach did summersaults. "Alone?"

"I can't make it this way. Toss me the lantern and go. I'll meet you at the rendezvous like we talked about.

Anya clutched the lantern handle so tight her knuckles turned white. She couldn't navigate the city alone, at night. Maybe during the day, but even then...

"Hurry, Anya, they're coming. I can't stay here."

She peeled her fingers off the handle and tossed it down. Fedor caught it and immediately set out up the tunnel. Anya turned to look back the way they'd come.

A pair of yellow eyes stared back at her. Her breath caught in her throat and she ran. Whatever she found in the city couldn't be worse than whatever was down there.

* * *

Fedor secured the lantern and ran. Every pounding stride jarred his aching arm, but he didn't care. He'd seen those glowing yellow eyes once before, when the Empire sent a dragon-blood to raid one of their meetings. There had been twenty rebels at that gathering, all of them armed and experienced men. Only Fedor and two others had escaped with their lives that day. He'd hoped to never see those eyes again, but it seemed he was out of luck.

The elite soldiers of the Empire could see in the dark as well as having their other senses enhanced. Their scales were tough enough to turn aside bullets and the less he thought about their sheer physical strength the better.

He needed to put as much distance between himself and the monsters on his trail as possible before they forced their way through the rockfall. At least Anya was safe for the moment. If the ladder rungs broke under his weight, no way could a dragon-blood follow her. He leapt a boulder and sighed. She was alone in a city filled with zealots hunting for her yet he was relieved she wasn't in the tunnel with him. The world had clearly gone completely upside down.

Behind him the crash of falling rocks alerted him to his hunters working their way through the barrier. It wouldn't take long. He'd seen the monsters rip a man completely in half with their bare hands. A few rocks wouldn't slow them for long.

Fedor winced at a particularly bad twinge and grabbed his arm. His hand came away wet. The wound had soaked through Anya's makeshift bandage. Not good. He was probably dripping a trail for them to follow.

He tore a strip out of his shirt and wrapped it around the wound, grunting when he pulled it tight. That should buy him a few minutes, maybe. What Fedor really needed was some way to throw them off the trail.

As he ran his mind raced. What could he use? His gun was useless against the monster's scales and he needed the lantern to keep from breaking his neck in the dark. That pretty much summed up his assets and he wasn't encouraged.

A loud squeak drew his attention. He shifted his lantern and found a fat brown rat with its paw caught between pieces of broken cement. Maybe he could lay a false trail. That would buy him a little time.

The rat bared its fangs as he approached, but Fedor grabbed it tight by the back of the neck and worked it free of the stone. He kept running, a rat in one hand and a lantern in the other. If anyone had seen him they'd have laughed, but Fedor wasn't in a laughing mood.

Fifteen minutes later he reached a three-way intersection. Finally, exactly what he'd been hoping for. He set the rat down and stepped on its tail. Next he tore of a strip of bandage and tied it around the rat's neck. A poke of his boot sent it rushing down the left tunnel. Fedor grinned and ran down the central passage.

* * *

Yarik stood at the base of the rockfall and stared up at Victor. They'd been chasing the fugitives through he didn't know how many miles of tunnel before reaching the barrier. He was thoroughly and completely sick of the dark, dank passage. The sooner they got to the surface the better. From his position at the top of the rubble Victor mumbled something, but his face was pointing away and Yarik couldn't make him out.

"What did you say?"

Victor pulled his head back and looked down, his eyes glowing in the dark. "They split up. The girl has returned to the surface and the man went down the tunnel."

"Can you get through?"

"I need to shift a few boulders, but it won't take long."

"Get on it." Yarik paced as Victor sent rocks tumbling down from the pile. Why would they split up now? Leaving the girl on her own was risky at best and insane at worst. He'd been so careful to keep her close, why leave her alone now? Maybe to force them to choose who they wanted to chase.

Victor tumbled down and crashed into the ground beyond the rockfall. "It's clear on this side!"

Yarik clambered up the pile, through the widened gap, and down beside the dragon-blood. Hedon joined them a moment later.

"Who do we chase?" Hedon asked.

"The girl of course. Get up there."

Hedon made it to the third rung before one snapped under his weight. Yarik eyed the rusty ladder. That explained why they split up. Anya made it up, but her heavier companion couldn't follow.

"Change of plans," Yarik said. "We follow the man and make him lead us to the target."

"That won't be a problem." Victor sniffed the air. "He's bleeding. We can track him easily."

The three hunters set out after their prey. Hedon and Victor ranged ahead while Yarik brought up the rear with his flashlight. Unlike the dragon-bloods, he couldn't see in the dark.

As they jogged through the tunnel he couldn't stop thinking about his wife, all alone in their little cabin. She had to be worried. He'd had time to let her know where he was going, but still he wished he had a chance to call and tell her he was okay. It would have been nice just to hear her voice.

He'd seen a lot of the Empire and its allies over the last few weeks and while he knew it was corrupt and self-serving, he never imagined the czar working with lunatics like Father

Gabriele. The priest would happily burn everyone and every-thing that didn't fall into line behind his mad church and that included the Empire. Since Yarik knew the czar wasn't a fool, that meant he was planning to betray the zealots before they betrayed him. The whole exercise left Yarik nauseous.

Hedon and Victor's snuffling was just starting to get on his nerves when they stopped. Yarik jogged up to join them. The tunnel branched in three directions.

"Which way?"

The dragon-bloods looked at each other then at him. "We're not sure," Victor said. "From the smell it's like he went in two directions, left and straight."

"How can that be?" Yarik asked, the first hint of a headache building behind his eyes.

"It can't," Hedon said. "Yet I smell it that way too. That's why we stopped. I don't know which one to follow."

Gah! Why couldn't anything be simple? "Go left. If we're wrong we can always backtrack."

Victor led the way and they were off. Yarik didn't know how long they followed the tunnel before it came to a rock-slide that filled it from top to bottom. A rat was nibbling some-thing brown and disgusting off to one side. A piece of cloth was tied around its neck.

Quicker than someone his size should be able to move, Victor grabbed the rat and sniffed it.

"The man tied part of his bandage around its neck to lay a false trail," Victor said. He squeezed, crushing the rat to pulp.

The hunters backtracked and hurried down the central tunnel. It seemed to run for miles. At the end they came to another platform with a set of stairs leading to the surface. They went out in the early morning light. There was no sign of their prey.

"Can you smell anything?" Yarik asked.

Hedon shook his head. "It's too open up here. The tunnels concentrated the scent. I'm sorry, Agent."

Yarik spun in a slow circle taking in the ruined buildings and pocked streets. He took deep breaths, trying to cool his rising anger. These amateurs were making them look like idiots. They needed to return to Calais quickly. The only advantage they held was knowing the target's ultimate destination.

* * *

Anya slunk along at the edge of the sidewalk, ready to duck out of sight at the first sign of movement. She clutched the pistol Fedor had given her like it was a talisman. The dawn light cast long shadows which at first had unnerved her before she realized that they were telling her how to get where she needed to go. He said the memorial was north, so judging from the direction of the shadows it didn't take much to figure out her path.

The silent, near-empty city gave her the creeps. Even back home there were more people than this. They'd studied the war between France and the Blessed Realm, but she no longer trusted much of what she'd learned in the Empire. Her time in the Land of the Night Princes had taught her the Empire tended to lie when it was convenient.

She paused at an intersection and heard voices. Part of her brightened at the thought of other people then the rest of her panicked since anyone she met could potentially want to hurt her. Better to avoid everyone until she caught up with Fedor.

A few paces behind her was a porch. She darted back and ducked behind it. She'd barely gotten out of sight when a group of four dirty kids about her own age, dressed in rags and carrying a mixture of hammers and pry bars came sauntering on by. There were three boys and a girl and they were chatting in French, at least she assumed it was French. Anya spoke Russian, or New Imperial as the officials called it, and English. If she'd known she'd end up wandering Paris on her own she might have made an effort to learn a little.

One of them looked her way and she quickly ducked down again. Please, keep going. She didn't want any trouble and she really didn't want to have to shoot anyone. Anya wasn't even sure if she could shoot someone when it came right down to it.

She held her breath and listened. The voices got softer and softer. She relaxed. They hadn't seen her.

Anya started to get up when a burst of machine-gun fire filled the air. She crept out from her hiding place and eased out so she could look down the street. A pair of men in black armed with rifles stood over the bodies of the four kids. Gold crosses hung from their necks so she assumed they were from the holy army, the last people in the whole world she wanted to deal with.

She ran back the way she'd come. Hopefully they hadn't noticed her.

From behind came the sound of pounding footsteps.

So much for hope.

A little ways ahead on her right was an alley with a dented dumpster. She ran down it and crouched out of sight. If they didn't see her maybe they'd think she'd kept running.

Anya slipped the safety catch off in case they didn't. Her heart pounded so hard she had trouble hearing the heavy tread of the soldiers' boots.

The thudding stopped.

"I'll check the alley and catch up with you," someone said in English.

Her hands trembled and her knuckles were white on the pistol's grip.

Soft steps approached. He crunched on some garbage. *Clang, clang, clang,* he tapped on the dumpster.

She held her position. The holy warrior appeared in front of her and Anya pointed the pistol at him, center mass like Fedor had taught her.

He laughed. "Do you even know how to use that thing?"

"Please just leave me alone," Anya said as tears ran down her face. "I don't want to hurt you."

He laughed again. "The way your hands are shaking I doubt you could hit me if you had the guts to shoot, which I also doubt. Why don't you lower that gun and come with me? It isn't safe out here for a girl on her own and the men at the barracks would be excited to meet you."

His leer sent a shiver down her spine.

"I'm not going anywhere with you. Now go away!"

He took a step toward her. "Don't be stu—"

Boom!

The pistol shot was deafening in the tight space. The soldier clutched his chest and stared at her in disbelief. He fell to his knees then landed at her feet.

Anya scrambled up and ran. She didn't have a plan, didn't think. She just ran, as far and as fast from the man she'd killed as possible.

When her lungs were burning and her heart pounding so that she feared she might collapse she found a smashed-in storefront and slipped inside. She just needed to catch her breath for a minute.

Glass crunched under her feet as she made her way deeper

into the shop. The shelves had been ransacked long ago. In the rear wall she found a door that led to small office with a table, chair, and battery-powered lantern.

She slumped into the chair and sighed. God, she was tired. Her legs felt like year-old rubber bands. It wouldn't hurt anything if she rested for a little while. Anya put her gun on the table and noticed whoever had stayed here before her had left behind an English newspaper. On the front page was a handsome young man of Japanese Imperial descent. She checked the date. Three weeks ago.

Desperate for anything to distract her from what happened in the alley she picked up the paper and started reading.

The world's first male wizard, Conryu Koda, proved himself a friend to the Alliance this week when he singlehandedly saved Sentinel City from a grim fate. The terrorist organization known as the Le Fay Society attempted to open multiple gates to the nether-world and only this brave young wizard was able to stop them. Many people are calling Conryu a hero, but the humble young man insists it was only with the help of his numerous friends that he managed to succeed in stopping the plot.

Whether he's simply being self-deprecating or not, this reporter is glad to know Conryu Koda is watching over the Alliance.

She shook her head and tossed the paper on the table. This boy, barely older than her, had saved an entire city. Surely if he could do that, then she could make the trip to the Eiffel Tower Memorial.

Heartened by the story, Anya pushed away from the table and took up her weapon. She was going to make it and no one would stop her.

Anya left the shop and retraced her steps, being careful to avoid the alley where she'd left the dead man. She made quick progress through the empty streets and half an hour after finishing the article found a sign that gave directions to the memorial and said it was a quarter mile away.

The memorial wasn't terribly impressive, it consisted of a simple black plaque with the inscription "Never Forget." She wasn't sure what they weren't supposed to forget. If it was the Elf War then it went without saying no one would ever forget. After all, nearly three-quarters of the world's population died before the elves were driven off or killed.

"Anya."

She spun and raised her gun. Fedor strode into the clearing. His shirt and pants were torn and his makeshift bandage soaked with blood. All in all he looked like he'd been through a war. Which she supposed he sort of had, a small one, but still bad enough.

Anya ran over and hugged him. "Are you okay?"

"Yeah. I think I finally shook off the monsters that were chasing us."

"Monsters?" She'd half convinced herself that the yellow eyes were a trick of the light.

"Dragon-blood soldiers, the Empire's elite. The czar is certainly determined to get you back."

Anya was equally determined to escape. For all this time she'd been running and hiding with no real goal of her own. But now she had one. She was going to meet the boy in the story.

* * *

Hedon and Victor had returned to their human forms when Yarik led them back to the subway entrance. They came by surface road after they finally found a way out of the underground. It annoyed Yarik to no end that he'd failed once more to capture the girl. It was like trying to tackle a greased pig, she just kept slipping through his grasp. He'd have one more shot at Calais. If they screwed up there, well, he didn't want to think about it.

"Agent Yarik!" Father Gabriele hurried toward him, a mad smile plastered on his twisted face. "We've had a glorious victory. The heathen frogs had no idea what hit them. We made a glorious slaughter in God's name. The Archbishop will be pleased and we have you to thank."

Yarik grunted. He was in no mood to celebrate with the god-drunk lunatic. He needed to return to Calais.

"I'm thrilled for you, Father, but we need to get back to the port as soon as possible. Our target escaped us and will surely make for her escape route as quickly as possible."

"Of course, of course. We're done here anyway." Gabriele turned toward his celebrating men. "Everyone on the bus. We're going home."

That brought another loud cheer and they all climbed aboard. The bus was nowhere near as crowded this time when they turned north. The zealots had lost two-thirds of their number yet they seemed almost high on victory. Perhaps they were happy for their dead comrades who got to go to Heaven ahead of them.

Whatever, Yarik was happy to be able to stretch his legs out and take a nap. He was so tired even Father Gabriele's driving couldn't keep him awake.

The next thing he knew Hedon was shaking him. "We're here, sir."

Yarik groaned and sat up. His neck hurt like the devil after sleeping in that awkward position, but he felt rested, at least a little bit. Now he had to figure out how the resistance planned to smuggle Anya out of the country.

Once upon a time a tunnel had connected France and the Kingdom of the Isles, but the elves had destroyed that early in the war. A boat was the only possibility. He'd set a trap near the docks. Hopefully it would work out better than last time. It was time to stop thinking like a lion and start thinking like a spider. He'd make a web and sit in it until he caught his fly.

8

ESCAPE

They bounced along the rough road to Calais in the little car Fedor hot-wired, leaving Paris in their rearview mirror. They made no effort to contact the army. Fedor didn't say anything, but from the tightness of his expression she figured he didn't hold out much hope for their hosts. Anya did her best not to think about them. In fact, she tried not to think about a lot of things. The soldier she shot in the alley being at the top of the lists.

Unfortunately, she couldn't get him out of her head. Every time she closed her eyes he was there, staring at her with his perpetually open, accusing eyes, his shirt stained red. Once she'd fallen asleep and he moaned, "Whyyyy?"

She tried to scream, "Because you wanted to take me back to your friends and rape me!" but instead she woke up panting.

Anya glanced at Fedor. He stared straight ahead, his face set in a grim scowl, his injured arm cradled against him. If anything, she thought he looked worse now than he had in the tunnels. That was saying something.

"Why are you doing this for me?" The question had dogged her since the day they fled their little house. If there was ever a time to ask, this was it.

"The resistance thought that by getting you out it would help spread the word about our cause. I told you that." He never took his eyes off the road.

"I know you did, but what I want to know is why you? Considering everything that's happened why not cut and run? It would be a lot safer for you."

Fedor heaved a great sigh. "Do you know how your father died?"

She flinched, taken aback by the sudden change of subject. "I know he was killed by the Empire, murdered on some mission for the resistance, but not the details."

"The night your father made that run it was supposed to be my turn. We rotated so no one took all the risks, but my wife had fallen ill and I needed to stay home to take care of her. Your father offered to make the run in my place. It should have been me that was killed, but it wasn't. His kindness ended him."

"I'm sure Dad didn't blame you," Anya said, "If Mom got sick you would have done the same for him."

"I would have, but it didn't work out that way and I had to live with my best friend's death. When the decision was made to get you out of the Empire if you passed your wizard's test, I knew what I had to do. I swore I'd get you to safety no matter what it took. And I will."

"What about your wife?"

"She died a month after your father. Cancer, they said. The witches don't waste healing magic on nobodies like us. I had always hated the Empire for its cruelty and oppression, but when they let her die when a bit of magic might have saved her..." Fedor shrugged and seemed unable to continue.

Anya watched the countryside go by for a few minutes. Away from the city France seemed more at peace. Perhaps the fields and forests hid the effects of the war better than the crowded buildings of the city.

Another bump rattled her teeth. Maybe they could call a truce and fix the pavement. It would be a better task for all these men than trying to kill one another.

"There's another matter we need to discuss before we reach Calais." Fedor seemed to have collected himself and his grim scowl was back in place. "The Kingdom agent we're meeting has a small boat tied to the twenty-seventh berth at the docks. It's called *The Wave Rider* and her name is Rebecca North."

"They sent a woman?"

"Indeed, Rebecca is one of their finest field agents, or so my contact says. I've never actually met her. The description I was given was, long dark hair, green eyes, jagged scar on her right cheek. She'll wait for another three nights, then leave, with or without us. Hold the wheel a moment."

Anya took the steering wheel while Fedor reached into his inner shirt. He came up with a two-inch-long thumb drive. When he held it out she took it and returned control of the car to him.

"That's what they want," he said. "All the intelligence the resistance has collected is on that drive. It's encrypted. She may require you to hand it over before she'll let you on the boat. It's perfectly fine if you do, but don't give her the password until they've given you everything you want. Once you tell them you'll have lost all your leverage."

"You keep saying I should hand it over and I shouldn't give

them the password. What about you? You'll be there with me, won't you?"

"I hope so, but that security agent didn't strike me as the type to just give up. I fear we may have to fight our way past him and his monsters. If it comes to that I may not be able to go with you."

A chill went through Anya. "Don't say that! We haven't survived this long together only to fail at the end. We'll escape, both of us."

He finally cracked a smile. "You have your mother's strong will, that's certain. You'll need it in the Kingdom. They're good people for the most part, certainly compared to the Imperials, but like any other government they won't hesitate to use you and throw you away when they're finished. Keep that foremost in your mind."

Fedor gave her the password and made her repeat it five times before he was satisfied that she had it memorized. They passed the rest of the journey in silence. Anya did her best to convince herself that Fedor didn't intend to sacrifice himself to save her.

* * *

Fedor pulled off the road half a mile from the city. Beyond it the ocean sparkled in the afternoon sun. Anya got out and stared at the water. She thought she could smell a hint of brine, but it was probably her imagination. Beyond that lay her freedom, or maybe just a new prison.

After what Fedor told her about the Kingdom government she'd begun to doubt it was much better than the Empire. On the other hand they were offering her escape and safety instead of hunting her down so they could make her a slave. Maybe she'd give them the benefit of the doubt.

The driver's side door slammed, jarring her out of her thoughts. Fedor rotated his injured arm and glared at the city as though it was an enemy.

"Do we have a plan?" Anya asked.

"I have two plans, but I can't make up my mind which one to try."

"Let's hear them."

"One, we ditch the car, sneak in, and try to reach the boat without getting spotted. Two, we drive like madmen through town and run over anyone that gets in our way."

"Can we swim to the boat, like in Anapa?" Anya asked. Neither of Fedor's plans appealed to her.

"We could, but I doubt they'd leave that route unwatched a second time. If the enemy spotted us we'd be sitting ducks in the water."

"We're going to have to sneak in then. No way could we drive in without getting shot."

Fedor grinned at her. "Correct. We'll make a general out of you yet."

Anya shot him a glare. "You knew what we were going to do from the start. Why the test?"

"I wanted to see if you'd learned anything." He gave her shoulder a squeeze. "You may not believe it, but you'll do fine in the Kingdom, with or without me. The truth is I hardly recognize you as the scared girl I rescued in the farmhouse. You've grown, become strong. I'm very proud, and your father would be too."

She sniffed, fought the tears, and lost. Anya hugged Fedor and cried into his chest. All the fear and uncertainty that had built up over the past weeks poured out.

When she got herself back together and wiped her cheeks she said, "Thanks. We ready?"

"Did you check your weapon?"

Anya slid the pistol from her belt, pulled the magazine, checked it, and slammed it into place. "I'm good to go."

He nodded. "You certainly are. Come on."

They set out toward Calais, avoiding the road and traveling through the lawns and rubble of the ruined suburbs. It was weird and felt like trespassing, but she suspected the people that had lived here were long past caring if someone walked through their lawn. Given how little remained of the neighborhood she doubted they cared about anything anymore.

From a distance they looked over the checkpoint that led into the city proper. Four men in black carrying machine guns stood around a pair of sawhorses that blocked the road. It looked like a flimsy setup to Anya.

"Maybe we could have smashed our way through," she said.

"Sure, but the noise would have alerted every holy warrior in the city. We wouldn't have made it ten blocks before an RPG blew us to smithereens. No, slow and steady is best."

"If you say so." She eyed the hundred yards of open field between them and the nearest building, a ruined, half-collapsed shop of some sort. "How do we get across that?"

"We crawl." Fedor fell to his stomach and inched his way forward.

Anya made a face, but followed. Halfway across the field a spider nearly the size of her hand crawled in front of her. She held her breath and it quickly crawled on its way. She continued on with a relived sigh. Anya hated bugs.

After the longest ten minutes of her life they reached the edge of the field. Fedor gathered himself and looked toward the soldiers. They'd broken out a pack of cigarettes and were laughing about something. She doubted they'd be laughing if their boss showed up right then.

"Let's go." Fedor sprinted for the ruined building and Anya followed on his heels.

No alarm went up so she started breathing again. "What next?"

"The docks. Be careful, I'm even more convinced it's a trap after seeing the lax perimeter security. They want us in the city."

Anya couldn't think of anything to say so they set out, heading north, keeping to the shadows and alleys. Twice patrols of armed soldiers passed them by and each time Fedor grew more tense. It was starting to infect her, though how she could get any more nervous she didn't know.

The quiet was driving her crazy. It seemed like she'd visited nothing but dead towns since she left the Empire. Only Germany had been lively, but that seemed like a long time ago. What she wouldn't have given for a cup of tea and a cookie in a nice little cafe. Just something normal.

Fedor grabbed her and forced her flat against the brick wall they'd been following. A truck that looked to be part tank rumbled down the street. It had a huge gun on its roof and an angry-looking man behind it. She'd been so wrapped up in her daydreams she hadn't even noticed it approaching.

"We're getting close," Fedor said when the tank-truck thing had moved out of sight. "You need to focus."

"Sorry, it's just hard to be on alert every moment. I'm tired and hungry and scared. I'm ready for this to be over with."

"It won't be long now. Just keep it together for a little while longer. An hour from now you'll be out on the ocean and the Empire will be nothing but a memory."

She badly wanted him to be right. How long had it been

since she really felt safe? It seemed like a lifetime ago. "I'm okay now. What next?"

"We need some way to flush out whoever's watching the dock. We can't count on anyone distracting them for us this time."

"What about a fire? We could torch a building and when they come to investigate sneak past."

Fedor shook his head. "Look around. No one would care if one of these dumps burned down. We need something a bit more drastic."

The approach of another engine sent them huddling tight against the wall. A moment later a pickup with a machine gun mounted in the bed drove slowly by, the man in the bed looking left and right.

"Maybe we could borrow that," Anya said.

Fedor drew his pistol and worked the action. "You read my mind."

* * *

Yarik hated stakeouts. He sat on a barrel behind a half-built boat and yawned. For the better part of the day—he wanted to say Saturday but he'd lost track—he, along with Victor and Hedon, had been hiding out at the dock waiting for the girl to arrive. He feared the zealots might catch her before he did. If those lunatics got their hands on her who knew what they might do, his warnings not withstanding. Having seen their half-assed security patrols he didn't worry about it too much.

No, Anya and her protector would find their way through the gaps and to the docks where he'd grab them and drag them back to the Empire where the girl would be transformed into a

White Witch and become an enforcer for the state, bound to the czar and his will.

He sighed and thought of Irmina. She hadn't been much older than Anya and under the veneer of her station was a scared girl. It might have been kinder if the transformation took away all their free will and made them into mindless puppets.

Tires screeched and a pickup came careening around the bend and powered toward the dock. It was one of the zealots' patrol vehicles, but he recognized the bearded man driving it. His prey had arrived at last.

Yarik drew his pistol as the truck got closer. He squinted against the glare on the windshield. Where was Anya? As far as he could tell the man was alone.

The rebels had proven adept at distraction. Was this another one? A trick to draw them out and give the girl a path to her escape route. No, he wouldn't abandon his charge at this late juncture. The rebel had something else in mind.

The rear of the truck fishtailed and skidded into the side of a warehouse. The front end buried itself in the building. A moment later the man staggered out and climbed into the bed. He charged the machine gun and let loose with a spray of fully automatic fire.

Bullets slammed into everything. A pair tore through the half-built ship he'd been hiding behind and pinged off the ground around him. Yarik scrambled behind the heavy steel barrel. That should provide him with a little extra protection.

He looked to where the dragon-bloods were hiding and pointed at the mad rebel. They nodded and stepped out from behind a stack of pallets. More rounds bounced off their scales. It didn't even seem to hurt them.

Must be nice, being bulletproof. It certainly came in handy

in this line of work. They strode toward the truck, flinching occasionally when one of the shots hit square, but otherwise unbothered by the spray.

When the machine gun finally went silent Yarik risked emerging from his hiding place. Victor and Hedon were halfway to the truck and the rebel was trying to climb out of the back with one arm. Yarik rushed from his hiding place and ran to join the pair. They needed him alive to find out where Anya was hiding. He didn't want them to get carried away.

The rebel finally made it to the ground and ran. He had a hitch in his stride, probably injured something in crash.

Victor and Hedon stopped near the truck and were sniffing the air. Yarik stopped beside them. "He's getting away."

"I smell someone else," Victor said.

Hedon nodded. "Yes, he's not alone."

Yarik looked into the wrecked warehouse. Something shifted in the cab and a terrified face peeked out. Bright blue eyes met his and he made a stupid decision.

He couldn't stand the thought of those eyes become pale and lifeless like Irmina's.

"Forget that," Yarik said. "He can lead us to the girl, but not if he escapes. After him!"

Hedon and Victor ceased their snuffling and ran after the rebel. Yarik glanced at the girl and nodded before taking off after his subordinates.

The rebel had gained ground, but with his limp had no hope of escaping the rapidly approaching dragon-bloods. He seemed to know it too. A big automatic appeared in his hand and he fired at Victor. The bullets were no more effective than the ones from the machine gun.

Hedon drew a deep breath and exhaled a blast of frigid air. Ice formed around the rebel's feet and he crashed to the pavement. Victor stomped on his weapon hand and Yarik heard the bone break.

The rebel shouted and pounded on Victor's leg to less effect than his gun.

"Stop struggling," Yarik said. "You've led us a merry chase, but it's over. Where's Anya?"

The rebel lay on his back and laughed. "Far from here if the universe smiles."

* * *

Anya's heart nearly stopped when the Imperial agent looked in her eyes. She'd been certain the game was up. That Fedor's sacrifice was going to come to nothing. Then he ordered his monster to chase Fedor down, nodded to her, and ran off. She hesitated to break cover, but what could he have to gain by letting her go only to capture her a few seconds later?

Finally she steeled herself, climbed out of the truck, and ran toward the dock. She didn't dare look behind her for fear of what she might see. Anya needed to be stronger and braver than she'd ever been. That's what he'd told her just before they got in the stolen truck.

The piers each had a shiny number nailed to them. She hurried down the line until she reached number twenty-seven. A slick black boat perhaps thirty feet long was tied to the pier. On the back it said, *The Wave Rider*.

"Hello? Rebecca?"

There was a rustle from inside and a dark-haired woman with hard eyes and a scar emerged on deck. She held a sliver pistol in her hand.

"Anya Kazakov?"

She nodded. "Imperial agents are just up the pier. We need

to leave now."

Rebecca made no move to let her aboard. "You have the information?"

Anya dug out the thumb drive and held it up.

"Give it to me."

"When I'm on board." Anya looked over her shoulder. Fedor couldn't buy her much more time.

Rebecca raised her pistol and pointed it at Anya's head. "The drive, now."

Anya shifted so the drive was dangling over the water. "You think your masters will be pleased if this goes for a swim? I am sick of people pointing guns and threatening me. Either kill me or let me aboard."

Rebecca grinned and lowered the pistol. "You've got guts."

She held out her empty hand and helped Anya aboard. The boat wasn't much more than a cockpit with a wheel, throttle, and some gauges. At first Anya thought there was a below-deck area, but she was wrong.

"Hold on." Rebecca cut the lines holding the boat in place, slid into the driver's seat, and turned the key.

The engine rumbled to life and sent a vibration through the hull. She thrust the throttle forward and they leapt away from the dock. The coast quickly grew smaller. This boat was faster than any of the cars Anya had ridden in.

When she mentioned it Rebecca said, "It's designed for smuggling people and weapons. At full thrust she'll make sixty knots. We'll have you to London in three hours. When we arrive you will have to hand over the drive."

"That's fine. You can have it now if you want. I was just sick of being threatened." Anya tossed the drive to her and Rebecca snatched it out of the air. "What exactly is on it and why does the Kingdom want me?"

Rebecca shrugged and tucked the drive away in an inside pocket. "Beats me. I just handle delivery. Once we reach London you're someone else's problem."

"Will you be delivering the weapons to the French army? The commander we spoke to seemed eager to get them."

"I'll deliver some of them. The rest will be brought by others. I'll tell you a secret. We would have provided them with the weapons they need even if the French hadn't agreed to help you escape. The last thing Downing Street wants is a country controlled by fanatics forty miles off our coast."

The sun slowly set as they made their way along the coast, eventually turning up a river. Rebecca wove her way through barge and boat traffic with ease. She brought them to a gleaming glass-and-steel building built right on the river.

As they drew closer Rebecca pressed a button on the control panel. A door in the cement wall slid open and she guided the boat through. A manmade canal ran a short distance to a private dock. Overhead bulbs filled the chamber with light. Two women, one in a red robe and the other in black stood flanking a slender man in a gray suit with salt-and-pepper hair and a neatly trimmed goatee.

The man smiled as the boat eased up beside the dock. "Anya Kazakov, welcome to His Majesty's Ministry of Magic."

"Thank you?"

He laughed, warm, rich, and inviting. He gave off an air of friendliness and good cheer. Anya immediately distrusted him. She'd never met a government employee that was friendly.

"I'm Agent Carter Smith, but please call me Carter." He held out his hand and helped her out of the boat. "I'm sure you've had a rough time of it. We'll get you settled in, perhaps a shower and a bite of dinner. I believe the kitchens prepared Shepherd's Pie. It's quite good."

Rebecca tossed him the drive, revved the boat's engine, and left the way she'd arrived.

Carter pocketed the drive. "She's a great smuggler, but weak on her people skills. This way."

He started up the pier toward the rear wall. Anya eyed the women then fell in behind him. They were probably the Kingdom's equivalent to White Witches. She'd have to be careful around them.

As her guide reached the end of the pier the blank wall slid open revealing an elevator. The five of them crowded in and Carter pressed a button. The car lurched and numbers lit up on a digital readout. When they hit six a chime sounded and the doors slid open.

Carter stepped out and they strode down a long, door-lined hall. He stopped again, this time in front of door number five and pushed it open. "It's not much, but I hope you'll make yourself at home. There's a shower and you'll find clean clothes in the dresser. I'll have the kitchen send up something for you in half an hour or so. Do you have any questions?"

"No, thank you."

"Have a good sleep. I'll fetch you in the morning. My superiors will have many questions not to mention there are a few tests we need to run."

Anya nodded, not really listening. Her eyes were locked on the turned-down bed in the middle of the room. A good night's sleep in a safe place would be heaven.

* * *

When Yarik heard the rumble of the engine he knew Anya had escaped. He should have been worried, terrified even, of his potential punishment, but all he could think was that he'd saved that girl from becoming a monster. Of all the things he'd done for the Empire, this failure pleased him more than any of his many successes. If someone had asked him to explain why, he wouldn't have been able to. It just felt right.

He looked down at the rebel who was still trapped under Victor's boot. Despite the pain of his broken wrist the man was smiling. He'd heard the engine too. There was a moment, not that the rebel would understand, that he felt a kinship to the man. In that instant, when he let the girl escape, Yarik in his own way became as much a rebel as the prisoner.

Hedon roared, shattering the silence of the dock. The dragon-blood reached down, grabbed the prisoner by the throat, and lifted him like he was nothing. "I'll kill you for this."

"Hedon, no." Yarik couldn't let his subordinate kill the rebel, not yet.

Hedon looked at Yarik and snarled, appearing for a moment more dragon than man. "Why not? He's worthless now."

"We still need to report our failure to the czar. Better we have a prisoner to hand over than face his wrath ourselves, don't you think?"

Hedon's expression twisted to one of fear. A perfectly reasonable reaction considering how angry their master was likely to be. "I hadn't considered that. You're quite right, Agent. Perhaps this worm's life will sate his rage."

He dropped the rebel like so much trash. The big man landed with a grunt, his face scrunched up in a pained grimace.

"Victor, you still have the communicator?" Yarik asked.

"I left it with our gear at the church."

Yarik nodded. "Grab the prisoner and let's go back. For better or worse, our work is done here."

9

CONSEQUENCES

Yarik sat bolt upright in the hard wooden chair and stared into the communicator. He was alone in the room he shared with the dragon-bloods, waiting for someone to answer his call. He held the cool, bronze mirror as far out as he could. Nosorova's glowing face eventually appeared in the glass. It didn't look quite so intimidating if he kept her at arm's length.

He'd spent the hour-long walk back to the church trying to think of a good excuse or even better several good excuses, for how the girl escaped. Another two hours of thought brought nothing better than the fact that he felt bad for her. Admitting that was the reason for her escape didn't seem like the best way to go. White Witches weren't big on sympathy. Yet another reason he was glad to spare Anya that fate.

"After all this time and effort, at the end you failed!" Nosorova's shriek hurt his ears, but he kept his expression neutral.

"Yes. How could I have known that her protector would

sacrifice himself to let his charge escape? He had to know the fate that awaited him if he was caught. No sane person would risk that."

"You have a point. Our agent in London reported her arrival at the Ministry of Magic fifteen minutes ago. We know where she is. It will be up to the czar whether we make another attempt to recover her."

Yarik seriously doubted the czar would be foolish enough to attack the Kingdom directly. So far the Four Nations' Alliance had been content to watch and occasionally provide weapons for their proxies like the French army. A direct attack would provoke a more aggressive counterattack. No, Anya was safe as long as she stayed in the ministry.

"Do you have any orders for us?" Yarik asked.

"Hold your position for now. His Imperial Majesty is meeting with his generals. When he decides how he wishes to proceed with this matter someone will be in contact."

She broke the connection and Yarik blew out a sigh. They escaped the ax, at least for now.

He set the mirror on the table and got out of his uncomfortable chair. Outside Victor and Hedon were waiting to hear their fate.

Yarik shook his head. "Sorry, guys. We're on standby while we wait for His Majesty to decide what to do with us. Might as well rest and recover while you can. Heaven knows where we'll end up next."

"The witch sounded upset," Victor said.

Yarik snorted. "The witches are always upset about something. I'm going for a walk to clear my head. It's been a long day."

"Do you wish us to join you?" Hedon asked.

"Thanks, but I'll be safe enough. I'm just going to wander around for a while. See you later."

Yarik left his subordinates in the hall and ambled down toward the chapel. The zealots were having their nightly prayer session so it would be a good chance to talk with the rebel.

Beyond the double doors to the chapel was a set of steps that led to the basement. Yarik descended, ignoring the cool, damp air. They'd rigged up a makeshift prison and torture chamber, or inquisition chamber as the holy men preferred.

He ignored the rack as well as the trays covered with sharp, pointy bits of metal. It didn't look all that different from the autopsy room at home, except for the fact that inquisitors preferred to work on the living instead of the dead.

There were three cells, though only one had an occupant at the moment. Yarik unbolted the thick oak door and stepped into the eight-by-eight room. The rebel was chained to the wall by heavy manacles that allowed him just enough movement to lay down on the flimsy cot that was the room's only furniture.

The rebel glared at him. "I suppose the torture is to begin now."

Yarik sighed. "No, we wouldn't want to risk any damage before the witches get a hold of you. I thought we might chat for a little while, you know, like civilized people."

He held up his manacled hands. "Yes, just like civilized people. Go away, Imperial. I have nothing to say to you and there's nothing I want to hear from you."

"She made it safely to the Kingdom, so our spies say."

The rebel finally sat up and took notice. "Anya's okay?"

Yarik nodded. "I thought you'd like to know."

His jaw bunched then he relaxed and offered a grudging, "Thank you. But why tell me?"

"I admired your sacrifice. Letting yourself get captured so she could escape took great courage. I doubt any of my fellow agents would be willing to make such a sacrifice. It deserved a reward of some sort, even a small one. I'm Yarik. You're Fedor, yes?"

"I know what you're trying, but it won't do you any good. As soon as I left the Empire the resistance changed all their meeting places and codes. You'll get nothing of use from me."

Yarik shrugged. "I don't really care about that. What you know or don't know is for your interrogator to determine. All I wanted to do was get to know you. See what sort of man you were. It seems you're a good one. Pity. I would have felt better about handing you over if you'd been a villain."

* * *

A hot shower combined with a full stomach and a good night's sleep could do wonders for a person. Anya snuggled deeper into the soft blankets. How long had it been since she slept in anything this soft? She managed to enjoy the feeling for almost a minute before she remembered Fedor, dead or captured in Calais. Much as she hated to think of him dead, Anya feared it might be the less-cruel option. She knew little about Imperial interrogation techniques, but she doubted they were pleasant.

Her throat tightened, but she refused to cry. He'd made the sacrifice for her and Anya intended to honor that, by showing these people how strong she was. That's what Fedor would have wanted.

Light poked in around the curtains so Anya got up and

threw them open. Beyond the window London sprawled as far as she could see. Tiny cars and tinier people rushed here and there. It looked alive. God it was good to see real people, happy, living normal lives, not hunkered down and under siege. Not a darkness-bound collection of undead or a terrified collection of regular folks afraid that a witch might knock on their door and steal their daughters away.

She jumped when someone knocked. There was a bathrobe hanging on the back of the door. She slipped it on and reached for the knob.

Carter stood outside. He smiled. "Morning. I trust you slept well, had everything you need, and all."

"Yes, thank you. The Shepherd's Pie was delicious."

"Told you. If you're up to it we'd like to get started with your assessment. Also there's the matter of the thumb drive password. We'll be needing it."

Now it was her turn to smile. "Perhaps when I've finished my assessment."

Carter laughed. "I like you, Anya. I think my boss will too. Why don't you get dressed and we'll get going."

Fifteen minutes later Anya walked into a lab where the woman in red from the night before waited. There were all manner of computers, microscopes, a weird machine with a digital readout and handles, and other items she couldn't identify from her six-month course in basic chemistry.

"Anya, this lovely young lady is Kimberly Kant," Carter said. "She's our Head of Magical Research. She'll be running a few tests on you to determine your magical capabilities as well as checking for anomalies in your blood. She's the best, so rest assured you're in good hands."

Kimberly walked over and waved her hands at Carter. "Shoo. We've got a lot to do."

"What about breakfast?" Anya asked.

"The blood tests give better results if your stomach is empty," Kimberly said.

"Don't worry, we'll get a nice brunch when you're finished," Carter said.

Kimberly pointed at the door and Carter shrugged and made himself scarce. Anya favored the wizard with an anxious look. "So what now?"

"Have a seat. We'll start with bloodwork then move on to power level and elemental alignment." Kimberly fished a small needle out of a holder while Anya took a seat on one of the stools. "Little prick."

Anya winced when the needle went in, but it wasn't terrible. When Kimberly had taken all the blood she wanted a cotton ball was taped to her arm.

"You're eighteen right?" Kimberly asked.

"Yes, ma'am."

"Excellent, we can't determine your element until you've turned eighteen. Don't ask me why, it's just the way it's always been. Step over to the machine and grasp the handles."

Anya hopped down, went over, and gripped the smooth, cold handles. Three seconds later the readout said 2500.

"Splendid," Kimberly said. "Well above average."

"What did the boy wizard get?" Anya asked.

Kimberly raised an eyebrow. "I'm surprised there was any mention of him in the Empire."

"There wasn't. I read an article in a paper while we were making our way across France. They made out that he saved an entire city on his own. It sounded ridiculous to me."

"It is ridiculous, it's also basically true. He did have some help, but Conryu Koda did all the heavy lifting on the mission himself. His power level is over 12,000. No ordinary wizard should compare herself to him. It would be like a torch comparing itself to the sun."

Anya didn't understand much about magic, but if her score was well above average what was 12,000?

"Okay, let's check your alignment." Kimberly brought out a frame holding six gems of different colors from black to white. "It's simple, just touch each gem in turn. The one corresponding to your aligned element will light up when you touch it."

"What was his alignment?" Anya touched the black gem but nothing happened.

Kimberly sighed. "Conryu is aligned to every element—don't ask me how that's even possible—but his strongest element is dark. Please continue."

She moved on to fire and struck out again. When she hit the brown gem it lit up like a light bulb.

"Earth aligned, interesting." Kimberly made a note on her pad. "Our research indicates that all White Witches are wind or water aligned and incapable of wielding fire and earth at all. This result argues that the process the czar uses to transform someone completely alters their magical flows. It's quite astonishing. I can't even begin to imagine how you'd do something like that."

"I'm not at all eager to find out."

"I expect not."

* * *

The numbers on the elevator climbed steadily as Anya and Carter rose ever higher up the building. Anya's examination finally ended after two hours of poking and prodding. None of it had been especially painful at least. When

Kimberly finally set her free she'd enjoyed a wonderful brunch with Carter.

After the last of the tea had been drunk he'd announced it was time to meet the boss. He hadn't been any more forthcoming despite her best attempts at coaxing. Perhaps it was a sort of intimidation. If so they'd have to do better. After everything Anya had been through, a little ignorance wasn't much of a threat. It was really more of an annoyance than anything.

"Can't you give me a hint about this meeting?" she asked.

Carter adjusted his red-striped tie and pursed his lips. "Sorry. My orders were very precise. The boss likes precision. And surprises. Don't worry, five more flo—"

An explosion rattled the elevator and they came to a stop.

"What was that?" Anya asked, her voice gone shrill with fear.

"Excellent question." Carter took out a small cellphone and pressed a button. "Ops, what's happening?"

A moment of silence and then, "Please repeat."

"What is it?" Anya asked.

Carter raised a finger to silence her. "Understood. How many? Okay. We're in the north-side elevator between floors fifteen and sixteen. I'll see about getting her somewhere safe."

He tucked his phone away. "We have a situation. The ministry is under attack."

"By what?" How could this be happening? She was supposed to be safe in the Kingdom.

"Dragon Manes, three of them as a matter of fact." Carter examined the elevator control panel and tapped the red emergency button. "A gift from the Dragon Czar no doubt. What I can't figure is how they got them into the city. We have excellent intelligence assets whose only job is to watch out for that kind of thing."

His calm was infuriating. "What's a Dragon Mane?"

Something buzzed and the door popped partway open. "Imagine if a dragon and a lion had a baby. Scales, fangs, wings, and breathes fire. Very tough. In fact, nearly impossible to kill without magic and only slightly easier with, they're highly resistant. Give me a hand."

He grabbed one side of the door and Anya got the other. They pulled and it slid open. They were three feet above the floor. He slid down then turned to help her. When they were both safely out of the elevator he looked around. Nothing in the red-carpeted hall looked promising.

Another explosion shook the building. "What now?" Anya wanted to run, but she had no idea where to run to.

"The safe rooms are all in the lower levels. We'll have to take the stairs."

Distant, muffled explosions sounded as they walked down the carpeted hall. Anya expected the passage to be filled with people running and screaming, but it was almost silent. They took a left and walked on.

"Where is everyone?" she asked.

"Emergency protocol is for regular employees to remain in their offices until the suppression teams have dealt with the threat. We don't need a bunch of people running around getting in the way. Ops says the monsters are on the third, tenth, and twentieth floors. So we only need to get past two of them to reach safety."

"Is that all?"

They reached a door and Carter yanked it open. Inside was a landing with a staircase running up and down. They went down.

After three flights a crash shook the steps and a loud roar echoed up to them. Anya leaned over the railing. Below them a hideous creature with golden scales and the face of a lion surrounded by a black mane looked up at her.

It opened its mouth and she leapt out of the way an instant ahead of a searing blast of flame.

"We need a new plan," Anya said.

Carter shouldered the door open and led her into another hallway. This one was lined with glass walls. People huddled under their desks. One woman started to get up when she saw them, but Carter waved her back. If Anya was the monster's target the last thing they needed was more noncombatants tagging along with them.

"How smart are these things?" Anya asked as they quick marched through the halls.

"I'm no expert." Carter glanced at her. "I work in human resources. My job is to orient new arrivals and make them feel welcome. My magical knowledge is extremely limited."

Movement from the right caught her eye. Outside the building one of the monsters was spitting fire at a figure in black robes who countered with a sphere of darkness. They were gone before Anya could learn the outcome of the fight.

"Who was that?"

He sighed. "My boss, the Ministry Chief. She's dark aligned and very strong. If anyone can deal with these invaders it's her."

They resumed their march toward wherever Carter was taking her. "Is she as strong as Conryu?"

"The boy wizard? No. I don't actually know her power level, but she's fought in several wars and acquitted herself well enough to get the highest magical post in the country. Here we are."

He opened a door that led to another staircase and they resumed their descent. On the fourth-floor landing the familiar crack of gunfire filled the air followed by a roar and screams of pain. Anya debated looking over the railing again, but decided to skip it.

Carter was looking from the steps to the next landing to the door to the fourth floor. Finally he flipped open his phone. "Ops, this is Carter. I need an update so I can get our guest to safety."

He glanced at her and Anya mouthed, "Put it on speaker."

Carter pressed a button and a female voice said, "The chief is engaged in a battle with one of the monsters and our rapid response teams are dealing with the others on the third and tenth floors. I have you on the fourth floor, correct?"

"That's correct, Ops. Can you give us a route to the safe rooms?"

"Negative, the third floor is a no go. You'll have to weather the storm on the fourth. Don't worry, we should have things in hand shortly."

The line went dead and Anya said, "Do you believe her?"

"Do we have a choice?" Carter countered.

* * *

As hiding places went, an office supply closet left something to be desired. Anya sat on a pile of printer paper across from her guide who had settled in on a broken-down copy machine. Every once in a while a roar or explosion would filter up to them, but otherwise they were in the dark as to how the battle was playing out.

"I don't suppose you can tell me the long-term plan for my time in the Kingdom?" Anya asked. She didn't really care at the moment, but she needed something to take her mind off the madness outside.

"I believe the plan was to have you attend King's College of Magic starting in the fall. As a defector you'll have all the rights of a full citizen. I understand it's an excellent school."

"Is it safe?" She gave their hiding place a meaningful look.

"You'll be surrounded by wizards. It's probably even safer than the ministry."

She snorted. "Talk about a low bar. They're never going to stop coming after me, are they?"

"The Dragon Empire? At some point it has to reach a point that the hunt becomes too expensive to continue. I assure you the king won't take this act lightly."

Anya knew he was trying to reassure her, but Carter really didn't understand the Empire. If the czar decided something had to be done, it wouldn't matter how much it cost or what the consequences were. He'd never stop until she was dead.

An especially loud crash sounded right outside the closet door. Anya looked at Carter who shrugged. She reached for the handle just as the door was ripped off its hinges.

The snarling face of a Dragon Mane stared at her from three feet away. An arm dangled from its mouth.

She scrambled away.

The monster opened its mouth and flames gathered.

She was going to die. Incinerated by a creature she'd never heard of miles from anyone she knew. She should have stayed home or with her mother and the vampires.

The Dragon Mane lurched sideways, twisted, and sent flames roaring down the hall. It charged down after its blast. The last thing she saw was its spiked tail thrashing and crushing the door frame.

"I'm alive." She could hardly believe it. Carter had moved to the doorway and peeked out. "What happened?"

"Kimberly." He had to shout to be heard over the blasts and

roaring. "She's fighting the Dragon Mane. I suggest we take advantage of her arrival and get out of here."

Anya was all in favor of that plan. She joined Carter at the door and risked a look down the hall. The combatants had moved out of sight, but the sounds of their fight still filled the hall. In the opposite direction was a gaping hole in the floor.

The monster had smashed its way through then tore a section of floor down to make a sort of ramp. Carter took her hand and they slid down together. A quick dash brought them through the rubble and to the stairwell. They ran down to basement level where Carter took her to a room sealed with a heavy steel door.

He grunted and dragged it open. The inside was like a one-room apartment. He motioned her in then pulled the door shut behind them.

"Will that door stop one of those monsters?"

"It will once I activate the security protocols." He removed an amulet from the front of his shirt and pressed it to the door. A flash of white made her squint then it was gone. "There. All the wards are now active. We'll be safe here while the Dragon Manes are dealt with."

"Safe," she muttered as she sat on the narrow bed. "I've heard that before."

* * *

Anya and Carter spent three tense hours in the safe room before the door opened. Standing outside was a woman in a black robe. A wisp of smoke rose from the tips of her tousled red hair and a streak of smeared soot ran down her pale face.

Carter leapt to his feet. "All secure, boss?"

She nodded, looking weary beyond words. "We lost forty people, mostly non-combat staff. When I find out who smuggled those Dragon Manes into the Kingdom I'll string them up by their ears."

Bright green eyes focused in on Anya. "I trust no harm came to you? I apologize that our meeting was delayed."

Anya waved her off. "I'm not going to complain given the circumstances. I'm sorry about your people."

"As am I. Perhaps we should take care of our business now. I'm Jemma St. Simon, head of the Ministry of Magic. It's a pleasure to finally meet you, Ms. Kazakov."

"Anya and thank you for taking me in."

Jemma offered a weary smile. "There, now that introductions are out of the way there's the matter of the password."

Anya winced. This probably wasn't going to go over well, but she had no choice. "About that. After this attack I'm not confident you can protect me. I want to be transferred to the North American Alliance and have Conryu Koda as my bodyguard. The most powerful wizard in the world should be able to keep me safe."

Jemma and Carter both stared at her. Well, let them stare. She'd made up her mind. A powerful bodyguard and an ocean between her and the Empire were the only things that would make her feel secure.

"It's not that simple," Jemma said. "We have a mutual aid treaty with them, but I can't just give an order and have them accept you as a refugee. Not to mention Conryu is a private citizen still attending their academy. I'm not certain what you're asking is possible."

Anya crossed her arms. "I'm sure their wizards are every bit as eager to study me as yours. You want the password, this is the price.

10

EPILOGUE

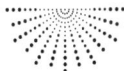

O rin Kane settled into his new chair and sighed. It had been a long day of meetings, but things were returning to normal in the Department after the madness of last month. He sighed, eyed the waiting pile of paperwork, and dismissed it. There was nothing that wouldn't keep until tomorrow. Maybe he'd head home early and surprise Shizuku and Maria.

He grinned and started to get up when his phone rang. Grumbling, he settled back and picked it up. "Yes?"

"I've got Jemma St. Simon on line two for you, Chief."

"The Kingdom head of magic? What does she want? She usually deals with Malice."

"I don't know, sir," his secretary said. "She just said she needs to talk to you."

"Okay, thanks." Orin pressed the flashing light on his phone. "Jemma? Orin Kane, what can I do for you?"

"I've got a problem and I think you're the best person to

help me with it. Are you familiar with the White Witch project?"

Orin wracked his brain but came up blank. With all the chaos over the past year he'd gotten behind on his station briefs.

"I can't say I am."

"It was a project to retrieve an untainted wizard from the Empire of the Dragon Czar. The mission was a success and the target, Anya Kazakov, escaped with a thumb drive full of secrets. Unfortunately the drive is encrypted and she's making demands."

"What sort of demands?"

Jemma gave him a brief description of the attack on Ministry HQ. "She's not confident we can protect her and I'm not sure I blame her. She wants to come to the Alliance and she wants Conryu as her personal bodyguard."

Orin winced. Conryu wouldn't be thrilled about that. Of course, he'd probably do it if the girl was in real danger.

"What are you offering in exchange?" Orin asked.

"I'll negotiate that with Malice. I just wanted to get you on board with asking Conryu since I know you two are close."

"Good call. If Malice asked or worse ordered him to do it, Conryu might tell her to stuff it. I'll talk to him. Conryu's a good kid. I suspect he'll be willing to help."

"Fair enough. Thanks, Orin." Jemma hung up.

Orin ran a hand across his face. So they needed yet another favor from Conryu. Well, at least he got to enjoy most of his summer vacation.

* * *

Yarik's legs ached. He'd been kneeling in front of the czar's throne for he didn't know how long. On either side of him Victor and Hedon had assumed identical positions. The czar had summoned them from Calais yesterday. The prisoner had been whisked away as soon as they arrived at the palace. Yarik did his best not to think about what Fedor might be enduring. Whatever it was he suspected it was far worse than sore knees.

He wanted to take a quick look around to see if he had any allies in the room, but didn't dare risk it. If he got caught looking before the czar gave permission it might mean his life. Better to remain ignorant and alive.

"She's gone!" the czar roared. His anger struck Yarik like a physical blow. "My witch has been sent to the North American Alliance. Sentinel City to be exact."

When no one spoke the czar asked, "How are we going to get her back?"

"Perhaps we should just cut our losses and let her go," a timid voice said.

There was a crunch followed by a thud. Yarik had heard enough bodies hit the floor to recognize the thud.

"Any other suggestions?" the czar bellowed.

"If she's been taken to Alliance territory, someone will simply have to go there and retrieve her," a woman, probably a witch, said.

"You three, on your feet."

Since Yarik and the dragon-bloods were the only ones kneeling they got up and faced the angry czar. Yarik bowed. "Majesty."

"It's your fault she escaped, so you three need to bring her back. I understand that that you have a wife, Agent. Rest assured, another failure will not be gently received."

"Of course not, Majesty." Yarik's mind raced as he tried to think of some way to talk himself out of having to go to the Alliance, but he came up blank. With the czar's unsubtle threat hanging in the air he had no choice. "Is there an entry plan? Their defenses are considerable."

The czar waved a clawed hand. "You'll travel by portal. No problem."

One of the witches standing beside the throne cleared her throat, leaned down, and whispered in the czar's ear. His frown grew deeper by the second.

When she straightened the czar said, "Isn't there some way around the defensive wards? There's no point in sending them if they're only going to get captured the moment they arrive."

"We're not aware of any, Majesty," the witch said.

"Perhaps I might be of assistance." All eyes turned toward the masked woman Yarik had noted in his last visit. If the regard of so many powerful people bothered her she gave no sign. "The Le Fay Society has located four blind spots in the Alliance's ward network where a portal can open with no one the wiser."

The czar tapped his chin. "And what would be the price of this information... Lady Wolf, wasn't it?"

"As I've said many times, Majesty, the Society desires better relations with your nation. We'd be happy to share one of our safe zones for your infiltration. Simply tell us where you wish to end up and I'll give you the nearest location."

A hint of a smile played around the czar's lips. "Perhaps I was too hasty in my assessment of your organization. Better relations might be in everyone's interest. You will work with Nosorova to come up with an infiltration plan. If it succeeds, well this might be just the beginning of our new relationship"

Yarik, Victor, and Hedon kept silent during this exchange. The thought of going to the Alliance worried Yarik no end, but if he wanted to survive he'd have to go through with it. He was no more eager to turn Anya over to the czar now than he was in Calais. Perhaps once he reached the Alliance he could defect. Maybe they could help him bring his wife over. Maybe someone would shoot him and put him out of his misery.

Right, and maybe he'd sprout wings and fly home. He just needed to accept the fact that right now it was Anya or his wife and if that was Yarik's choice then it was no choice at all.

* * *

Fedor hurt everywhere. He hung from a set of manacles the dangled from the ceiling of the Imperial palace's dungeon. No one had tortured him, which was both a surprise and a relief. It was coming though, he knew it. At least Anya was safe. Why the agent had bothered to tell him he couldn't say, but it was good to know. She was smart and tough; she'd make it in the Kingdom, he had no doubt.

He lifted his head and tried to see through the narrow slot in the door. There was nothing but a tiny rectangle of dull orange light. He'd been barely coherent when the dragon-bloods had brought him here, but he remembered torches and coal braziers. There didn't appear to be any electricity down here. It was probably an intentional way to ramp up the fear. It might have worked if he wasn't so exhausted. He hadn't had a proper night's sleep since they reached Paris days or was it weeks ago? He'd lost all track of time.

The light from the door vanished and a voice said, "Fedor?"

He didn't recognize whoever spoke beyond the fact that it wasn't the agent. He managed a groan.

"The Manager sends his congratulations. Anya has been moved from the Kingdom to the North American Alliance. The Empire made an attempt on her and she demanded they move her before she gave up the password."

Fedor smiled causing his blistered lips to split. She'd remembered his lesson. Good girl.

"I've been sent to offer you release if you wish it."

Fedor understood at once. Release, not escape. "Please."

"You've served the resistance well, brother. Your name will be remembered."

Fedor sighed and thought of his wife. He didn't know if there was a heaven, but if there was it would be nice to see her again. He flinched when something struck his chest then everything went dark.

* * *

Lady Wolf left the throne room when the Dragon Czar dismissed everyone, well pleased with her day's work. For weeks she'd been trying to find a way into the czar's confidence and now she'd finally done it. Who would have thought that child's escape would serve as the catalyst to her victory? It amazed and often frustrated her how much luck was involved in any given success.

But no matter. She quick stepped it back to the suite she'd been given for the duration of her visit. Her steps echoed through empty halls of the guest wing of the palace. No great surprise there since few people visited such a hostile nation. As far as she knew they didn't even have diplomatic relations with more than a handful of nations.

She rounded a corner and found one of the White Witches standing beside her door. She had a hard time telling them apart, but she was pretty sure this was the one that whispered in the czar's ear, Anastasia, the leader of their order.

Lady Wolf bowed. "What a nice surprise. I hadn't expected any visitors."

Anastasia closed the distance between them. "I don't know what game you're playing here and I don't care. If you lead His Majesty astray, I'll see you hanged by your guts from the palace walls."

Lady Wolf smiled behind her mask. So, this one already feared her influence with the czar. She'd made a better impression than she'd hoped.

"Let me assure you that everything that I've said and done has been in His Majesty's best interest. The Society truly wants better relations with your nation." That wasn't all they wanted of course, but no sense pointing that out until the time was right.

"We shall see and I will be watching." With that last threat Anastasia stalked off.

Lady Wolf shook her head and ducked into her room. Such blunt and obvious threats lacked subtlety. Crude though she may be, Lady Wolf had sensed Anastasia's power and had no desire to face her in a duel.

A swirl of her hand activated the anti-spying wards she'd set up the day of her arrival. Confident that she wouldn't be overheard, Lady Wolf went to the full-length mirror hanging in the bedroom and chanted.

Clouds filled the smooth glass and a short time later Lady Dragon appeared. "What news, Lady Wolf?"

"I have finally begun to win his confidence. I fear it's still too soon to ask for a favor, but when the opportunity presents itself I'm certain I'll be able to persuade him to do what we want."

"Excellent. We can't begin the next stage of the project without the artifact fragment. You're certain simply seizing it wouldn't work?"

Lady Wolf imagined fighting the czar and all his witches and shuddered. The entire Society wouldn't last five minutes. "No, the only way we can get the artifact is for him to give it to us willingly."

"I respect your judgement," Lady Dragon said. "Do what you must to secure it and do it quickly. Lady Tiger has a lead on the second piece. I want to be able to move as soon as she confirms its location."

"I'll do my best, Mistress." Lady Wolf bowed her head.

When she looked up all she saw in the mirror was her reflection. She'd made the first step, time and circumstances would decide when she could take the second. When the opportunity presented itself she'd be ready. Lady Wolf wouldn't fail the Society or their imprisoned leader. She would see Morgana freed regardless of the cost.

AUTOHER NOTES

I hope you all enjoyed reading about a different set of characters. I certainly enjoyed writing about them. Don't worry, in the next book Anya meets up with Conryu and more danger ensues. Until next time.

Thanks for reading,

James

ABOUT THE AUTHOR

James E. Wisher is a writer of science fiction and Fantasy novels. He's been writing since high school and reading everything he could get his hands on for as long as he can remember. This is his fourteenth novel.

www.jamesewisher.com
james@jamesewisher.com

Made in the USA
Middletown, DE
20 August 2021